Fish Ser

MW01036037

Fish Sergeant

by

John O. Pasco

College Station, Texas

ILLUSTRATIONS

by

Gertrude Babcock

Sonora, Texas

Texacornucopia Press

Longview, Texas

This book is dedicated to all generations of "Fish" of Texas A. & M. Who conceive and perpetuate its animating principles and form the essence of the legendary Aggie "Twelfth Man".

Foreward

The maxim "the more things change, the more they stay the same" relates to Texas A&M traditional mold that generates the Spirit of Aggieland. No longer is this legendary institution known as A&M, a diminution of Agricultural and Mechanical", but simply A&M; no longer is it necessary for the Aggies to select a sweetheart representative annually from their sister school, T. S. C. W. For now, thousands are chosen daily from its student body (since it is coeducational). Nonetheless, with each new generation of Aggies, the Spirit of Aggieland abides, which includes as one of its objectives the nurturing of first year students into mature ladies and gentlemen. Such a year of experience is witnessed in this book "Fish Sergeant."

This book is one you will enjoy from the first page to the last; not for the reason that you will find it a bit of literary excellence certainly, but because in it you will discover some experience almost your own! "Fish Sergeant" is a collection of letters, supposedly written from A&M College by one Elmer Hook, who began his life as a freshman in that school under the handicap of having been elected to serve as "Fish Sergeant" by the upperclassmen in his Battery. These letters take Elmer Hook through his "Fish" year at A&M from the first dissatisfied day until the time when he goes home for the summer holidays. Through these letters, it has been our endeavor to show that such qualities as discipline, honesty, loyalty, fair play and a sense of humor have been developing in "Fish" Hook as the indirect result of his association with other students on the A&M Campus, and that they are the necessary basis on which he will build the remainder of his college career.

Some of the letters are purely fictional, but the majority have been based on actual experiences as reported by various students of A&M. In following the course of outstanding events of the past school year from the point of interesting reading, we have tried to stress the oldest traditions and customs to which the corps adheres so strictly.

When Final Review is held in 1943 and Lieutenant Hook bids farewell to his comrades of four years, he will carry with him fond memories of his first trying year at A&M.

You will read "Fish Sergeant" in a very short time — but the memories will linger on for a long, long time. "Fish Sergeant" will surely have its own permanent place on the bookshelf of all Texas Aggies. It will not be out of place in any one's collection of interesting books.

William W. Chinn, Longview, Texas

Roy D. Golston'42, Ft. Worth, Texas

September, 1995

Fish Sergeant

ACKNOWLEDGEMENT

The author wishes to acknowledge his gratitude to the "Fish" who have assisted in the collection of the material used herein. He also wishes to express his thanks to Cadets Bill Murray, George Fuermann, "Jeep" Oates and other members of the staff of THE BATTALION for permission to use articles appearing in the student newspaper.

The author sincerely thanks Cadet Jack Littlejohn for permission to use the words to the chorus of his song, "I'd Rather Be A Texas Aggie." The author is also indebted to Howard Berry, Photographer of the Experiment Station, for the permission to use his photographs and to Professor F. ". McDonald, Head of the Journalism Department and Director of Publicity at Texas State College For Women in Denton, Texas, for the use of his photograph of the Chapel In The Woods. To all other contributing directly or indirectly to the letters collected herein, the sincere gratitude of the author is hereby expressed.

JOHN O. PASCO
College Station, Texas,
May 1940.

Fish Sergeant

Fish

Sergeant

Fish Sergeant

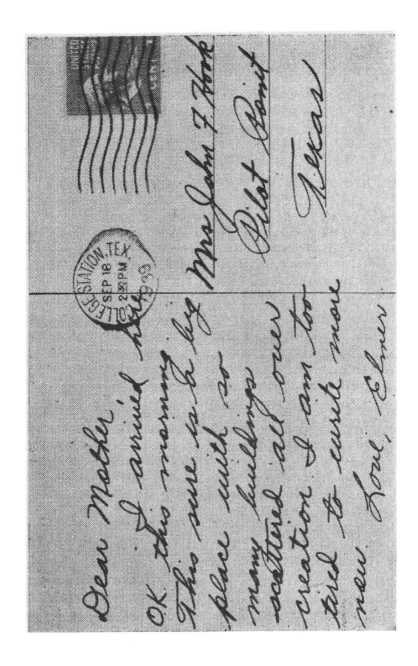

College Station, Texas

September 20, 1939

Dear Bill:

I arrived at this little dump a little before noon day before yesterday, and have been having hell ever since.

While I was on the train coming down, I met a boy from Dallas who is going to school here and is classified as a Junior. He told me I would have hell my freshman year, but that I would be well repaid for my trouble if I stuck it out. He said the upperclassmen gave the "Fish" the devil while they were on the campus, but would be the best friends when they were off of it or in years to come. I really do believe it because he sure was swell to me.

As soon as we got off of the train, Mr. Brown, the fellow I have just mentioned, took me to the new hall and we got there just in time to eat dinner. By golly, I never saw so many boys in all my life. Every place you looked there was a bunch of boys and they were all laughing and seemed to be having such a swell time. As for me, I would rather be at home, but I guess I'll get used to it later on.

After dinner, I found the place I was to stay and meet "My Old Lady" (roommate) and we shot the bull for the rest of the evening.

Yesterday morning, I got up real early and started out to register. I thought that if I got started fairly early, I could get through in an hour or two and have the rest of the day off. When I found the place to start, there was a line about a hundred feet long already formed and I had to wait about an hour before I got anything done. After this, I went from line to line, spending about an hour or two in each one. Several times, after having waited an hour or more, I would find I was in the wrong line and that meant having to start at the end of a new line. I finally finished registering about six o'clock. Boy, was I tired! And the blisters on the bottoms of my feet didn't help my disposition any, either. I finally got back to the room, and just as I got there, I was met by a bunch of pee-heads (Sophomores) who had several other "Fish" in tow. They began to tell us how dumb we were, and then gave us the rules as to just how we were to wait on the upperclassmen. To emphasize the importance, they sent the board around once and after this "woodshed feat," we were allowed to go to supper.

Right after supper, the pee-heads announced that there was to be a yell practice that night and everyone had to go. Boy, I hated to go because I was so tired I thought I'd drop, but there was no choice in the matter.

The yell practice was held in front of the Y.M.C.A. building and there was the "durndest" crowd of boys there I have never seen or ever hope to see, and we were packed in like a can of sardines. Pretty soon, the band started playing and everyone started yelling. We gave a few of the school yells and all of the football players were introduced. After the yell practice, I went home all tired out, but I think maybe I'll like this place after all.

It's getting late, so I had better close

Your friend,
Elmer

College Station, Texas

Sept. 26, 1939

Dear Bud:

I suppose every freshman at A&M as well as any other school has his troubles during the first few weeks at school. If I live to be 80 years old, I'll never forget my first experiences here, especially my first night in the dormitory. While I was unpacking my trunk on that never forgettable first night, I was surprised to see a bunch of boys burst into my room. One of them asked me my name, to which I replied, "Fish Hook." He thought I was just trying to be funny so he made me "duck waddle" around the room. Now, you know I couldn't help it if my name happened to be Hook, and I finally convinced him that my name was Elmer Hook for the one reason that I was Mrs. Hook's little boy!

After I had produced conclusive proof that I should be called "Fish Hook," I was told in no uncertain terms to find a Sophomore. They all looked alike to me. So in the process of finding a Sophomore, I asked several Juniors and Seniors if they were by chance Sophomores. By the time I found a genuine "soph," every upperclassman on that floor was "bleeding" at me. They all fell in line behind me, and followed me down the hall to give me a few pointers on how one might recognize an upperclassman. I thought I was in for it, but to my surprise, they went to work on the Sophomore, bleeding at him because we "Fish" were not on "the line." Of course, this didn't create any love for me in the heart of that particular Sophomore, so he held a special blood meeting for me. To impress me with the seriousness of the situation, I had to drink several glasses of hot water, do knee bends and push ups, hold up the wall, and stand on the little red stool. I also got a lesson in how to play "peek," and after I spent about an hour being told how low I was, I was allowed to find my way to bed.

My first meal in the mess hall was a treat too. The Aggies started saying: "Shoot the sky," "shoot the dope," "shoot the baby," etc. I was really in the dark. It was worse than facing an array of silver at a formal banquet — you know, that helpless feeling. So I just looked on for a while to see what it was all about. An upperclassman asked me for the "blood," but I had no idea what he wanted so I pretended I didn't hear him. After a strained silence, he yelled out: "Fish Hook, get your damn head out!" This about scared the wits out of me, so I ducked out of the mess hall pretty soon and to my room. I spent the afternoon with my Student's Handbook, memorizing everyone of the A&M nicknames. Here are some of them:

Prexy	Our President
O.D.	Officer of the Day
Soupy	Mess Call
Sawdust	Sugar
Shotgun	Peppersauce
Sand	Salt
Dope	Coffee
Cush	Dessert
Worms	Spaghetti
Sky-Juice	Water
Sons-of-Rest	Non-Military Student
Shot	Peas
Bull Pen	Informal Gathering of Students in Dorm
Cut	Desertion from Class
Gripe	Grouch
Dago	Macaroni
Fish	Freshman
Spuds	Potatoes
Blood	Ketchup
Rocks	Ice

Bull-Text	Military Science
Bull	Commandant
Ram	Demerits
Cackle	Eggs
Busted	Reduced to Ranks
Rabbit Food	Lettuce
Mealhound	Hearty Eater
Gun Wadding	Bread
Winchester	Soldier Out of Luck
Bull Flunkey	Worchester
S. O. L.	Orderly
Scabs	Post Toasties
Drag	Personal Influence
Shovel	Tablespoon
Horizontal Engineering	Napping
How do you rate that	What entitles you to that
Axed	Bested
Carried out in a gale	Bested in Conversation
Goldbricker	Carefree Student

Our Battery held a bleed meeting that night at which time we "Fish" were told that we would have to wait until all the upperclassmen had their plates filled with everything they wanted before we could eat, and that we could not eat "cush," unless they gave us special permission. It gets pretty tough when we have to pass up banana cream pie but that's just a freshman's life. Guess all of this sounds like fantastic tripe to you but "Fish" like it. We know it's been the same for every freshman in years past, and it makes us feel like we are becoming a part of the tradition of Aggieland. I like to feel it anyway — that I'm even a small part of the best school in America! I'll write to you more about the Aggie traditions next time.

Regards, Elmer

College Station, Texas

Sept. 30, 1939

Dear Bill:

I have been planning to write you for the past two weeks but it seems that we "Fish" are kept busy all the time. We have to learn every boy's name in our Battery, where he is from, his course of study; in fact, everything about him. We also have to learn all the yells—so you can see I have been busy.

Bill, do you remember I told you that my experience in the Boy Scouts would help me here at A&M? Well, I believe it is going to help me be made a sergeant. I certainly hope so. Our Battery is short of sergeants so the juniors and seniors are holding competitive exams for the vacancy. They are going to select one from the class. I was interviewed today by a court of juniors and seniors. They first selected about ten of us outstanding freshmen and had each of us come into the Captain's room for questioning. The court was very impressive. When I first came in, all of the upperclassmen present stood up and introduced themselves. They were dressed in No. 1 uniform. The room had one chair in the center of a large ring of chairs. The Captains asked me to take the center chair, and then called the court to order. The Court Recorder took my name, age, rating in high school, previous military training, etc. After he had gotten all of this information, the lights were turned off and a flash light was shined on me like a spotlight. Each junior and senior asked me questions. I would tell you what some of them were, but I am not allowed to repeat them. I think the court was very much pleased with me for I was kept much longer than any of the other boys and when my interview was over, the Captain had the court adjourn and I was dismissed.

I will let you know how it turns out. Please don't tell the folks as I want it to come as a surprise—that is, if I get the promotion, and confidentially, I believe it's in the bag!

My course is very interesting. I haven't had a chance to settle down to studying but I can see it coming soon; the need to study for Quiz A.

Well, be good and mum's the word until you hear from me. Don't know to what particular thing I should attribute my good fortune, but it may have been that the Captain liked the looks of those pictures I have of Ellen, Sue, and Emmy Lou. I have them hanging on the wall above my desk, with all my medals, ribbons and stuff like that tacked above them. Makes a kinda' nice display, especially with the Boy Scout Medal hanging at the top.

I'll let you know how it comes out.

Regards,

Elmer

College Station, Texas

Oct. 2, 1939

Dear Mom:

I have great news for you. I HAVE BEEN ELECTED "FISH SERGEANT!" It all happened like this:

There was a shortage of good sergeants among the upperclassmen, so they had to select one from the "Fish" — hence the name, "Fish Sergeant." The juniors and seniors had a court in the Captain's room the other night and interviewed several of us prospective "Fish." And I was selected out of all of our Barracks!

I will have the same authority as the juniors and can even make the seniors keep order if they make too much noise. It is an honor and all the "Fish" were trying hard for the job.

This morning at Company formation, the Captain called me out in front of the Company and pinned sergeant's stripes from the shoulder to the cuff of my left shirt sleeve. He announced my duties and told me he was counting on me personally to help him keep order. Kinda made a lump come in my throat, and I could hardly make my acceptance speech. Makes a guy sorta feel touched to know that the upperclassmen put so much faith in his ability, and believe you me, Mom, I'm going to do my best to live up to their trust.

I was given an end position in the front rank where I could better watch the boys. At noon today, I had to make a speech over the loud-speaking system in the Mess Hall pledging my word as a "Fish Sergeant" to do my best to keep order in my Battery and on the Campus in general. I really got a big hand when I sat down.

It is now nearly one and I have a class to make. I took time out to write you the good news. I'll write more later as I know you're going to be anxious to know that I'm making it good.

Love to all,
Elmer

College Station, Texas

Oct. 8, 1939

Dear Bill:

Boy! I made it. You'll have to address your letters to "Fish Sergeant" Hook now. The company Captain told me he was sure I would make the best "Fish Sergeant" the school ever possessed.

It all happened yesterday. I was called out in front of the Company and given my sergeant's stripes and a ram book as well as my instructions. Well, I have already had to exercise my authority on two juniors. They got into a fight over a girl. I heard them and ran to stop the noise. Somehow, I seemed to have made them sore at me for they both turned on me, and I was pretty bruised up, but I finally stopped the fight. They both looked sorta amazed when I put up a stiff battle, but I let them know I was there to preserve order and that I meant business. In about ten minutes everything was quiet again. Bill, you know how hard I am to get mad! Well, this little incident almost made me sore. I can see right now that I am going to have trouble, but the Captain sure won't be able to say that I didn't help all I could.

I reported the names of the two juniors to the Captain and he told me to really tear into the next fight and stop it right away. Believe you me, I'll show 'em!

Well, it's now C.Q. (Call to Quarters) and everyone is studying. I have some math . . .

I was interrupted there—about an hour ago! Of all the d— — fools I ever saw! I believe we have the schools worst in this Battery. It is now 10 o'clock and all I have done the past two hours is keep order. I have two pages of names to turn in to the Captain. C. Q. Is the study period when everyone is supposed to be in his "Hole" studying. I started to study my math when hell seemed to break loose down the hall and someone yelled for me to come stop another fight. Well, I waded in with both fists flying and stopped this one in short order—only to have an argument break out at the other end of the hall. As a peacemaker, I'm more over worked than Chamberlain, but I sure get more done! By the time I had the fellows quiet in that end of the hall, somebody squared off across the aisle and I had to stop that fight. From the number of fights we have in this Battery, one would think it a gathering place for possible "Dead End Kids." Guess it's the old power of suggestion, for it seems that every time a fight starts, it leads to another and I'm getting plenty tired of it already.

I'm going to bed now as I am too tired to study. I'll let you know more later on, but I'm going to put a stop to this foolishness if it takes me two months to do it. Boy, I didn't know what a job I was taking on!

Your friend,
Elmer

College Station, Texas

Oct. 9, 1939

Dear Bill:

Boy, what a weekend. I hitch-hiked to our sister school, Texas State College for Women, in Denton. I had been hearing so much about the beautiful girls that abound on the campus of the largest college for women in the United States that I decided to conduct a little inspection trip of my own. I had been told that one merely had to walk on the campus with his A&M uniform and a date was in the making. I was rather dubious of this statement, so I decided to get a proper introduction by one of the upperclassmen whom I had met on my way. We went to Lowry Hall where I was introduced to a "prison-mother" lady attached to a pair of search light eyes that took a ten cent shine off my shoes and tarnished my brass. They (the eyes) took our names and asked us what we wanted. If I had answered truthfully, I would be a life-time member of their black list. The upperclassman came to my rescue by asking for a couple of girls whom he knew. After what seemed two eternities, the girls came tripping down the stairs. Such lovely curvaceous blondes. I know I blinked my eyes for several seconds before I muttered some form of acknowledgment to their merry "How do you do." My friend explained that this was my first trip to TSCW and that I wanted a date, so he arranged things with Jane and he left with his girl, leaving me in the midst of all those girls. Seeing that I was ill at ease, Jane suggested that we take a stroll over the Campus before we took supper in the dining hall. I told her I would agree to the stroll, but the eating in the dining hall was out. How can you argue with two searching blue eyes, especially when they belong to a gorgeous blond with whom you are trying to make a hit? So with many misgivings, I was persuaded to endure the torture of a meal in the dining hall of the largest girls' school in America. As I very sheepishly descended the stairs (the dining hall is in the basement of Lowry Hall), a pink color started on my ears and rapidly spread over my whole face. Missing the two bottom steps, I made a very awkward entrance, and of all times to make such an entrance — with over a thousand beautiful eyes focused on me. After swallowing my heart two or three times, I finally managed to seat myself and habitually tucked my napkin under my chin, then blinked and gazed stupidly around completely unaware of the cause of the girls' mirth. One very kind soul finally whispered the answer to the question my eyes were obviously asking. Jerking the napkin out, I tried to hide my face in my plate but I was unable to concentrate on my eating for all the talking that was taking place around me. Judging by the food they place before you, one would be led to believe the girls were all dieting. I never saw such dainty helpings as the girls took on their plates. I tried to follow suit the best I knew how. You can imagine how hungry I was after hitch-hiking all day on one sandwich and one coke. I had barely begun to eat when the waitress took my plate away from me. What an ordeal — I know I must have committed mental suicide a thousand times before we left the table. And I was still hungry enough to eat my belt.

The meal over, my date and I checked out for the College Club for an evening of dancing. My date signed a big book near the door — another requirement. The dance hall was so crowded and the night so balmy, I suggested we stroll in the park. The next day I was to discover what a beautiful park we visited, but during that stroll under the moon-bathed trees and over the soft, thick grass I was aware of nothing but her presence and my utter lack of words. You know, Bill, I am no slouch when it comes to courting the girls, but somehow this girl was different. I just could not find the right words to lead up to anything. This girl had been around and she really knew how to carry a conversation away from one subject to another. We finally stumbled upon a lily pond that I could faintly see outlined in the shape of the State of Texas. There beside the water with the moon shining through her hair, I could not resist the temptation to take her in my arms. She resisted furiously as I kissed her luscious lips hungrily, not once but many times. When I turned her loose, she sank to the ground and cried as if her heart would break. You can imagine how I felt as I tried to comfort her. The more I talked the more she sobbed, so I just stopped talking and let her have her little cry. It seemed that she would never stop crying. Finally she ceased and apologized for being such a baby. She then told me that she had promised her boyfriend back home that she would not allow an Aggie to kiss her while she was away at school. It seems that the Aggies have a reputation for stealing other boys' girls away from them. I told her I was sorry I had caused her to break her promise to her boyfriend, but I was glad I kissed her. She didn't seem to like this remark so much, so we started back to the dance hall. I told her to wait a minute as I ran back to the pond and dipped my handkerchief in the water and gave it to her to wash her face. She seemed to appreciate my thoughtfulness for she was actually laughing again after she dried her face with my second handkerchief and had applied the proper amount of cosmetics.

We danced until it was time to return to the hall — eleven o'clock. I made a date for the following morning — and do you know what, she actually took me to church. Boy, I tell you there is just something about her that is different from most girls. She told me when I left that we could be good friends but nothing else, so I guess you would say I just spun my wheels on my first trip to the haven of beautiful girls. I don't think so, for I met some other cute tricks and besides, I may be able to make her change her mind.

Write,
Elmer

College Station, Texas,

Oct. 9, 1939

Dear Mom:

You shouldn't have had the *Record* print that I was promoted to "Fish Sergeant" here. I know it is an honor and all that, but I'm afraid it's going to cause me some embarrassment. One of the boys in the Battery saw the article in the paper over at the Library and cut it out. It has been tacked up on the bulletin board in the Academic Building for two days now. Some of the fellows have been razzing me about the publicity already. But I think they're just jealous and are trying to make trouble.

I've been trying to get down to my studies. There's so much responsibility to this sergeant business, though, I don't have time to study much. I hope the fellows will settle down pretty soon and quit trying to have too much fun. Seems like the upperclassmen are the worst of the lot — they never seem to have a serious moment.

I'm liking this place fine, Mom, so don't worry any about me. I'm sure I can make the grades. I sure would like to go down to the post office one day next week and find a box of your nut cookies in the mail. How about it Mom?

Love,

Elmer

College Station, Texas

Oct. 12, 1939

Dear Bill:

Something terrible has just happened. A little while ago one of the upperclassmen murdered another boy in the Battery. I actually saw the body — blood was all over the place. Many things have happened since I came over here, but this is the last straw. I'm coming home tomorrow morning early. We are afraid to leave our rooms now that it's dark.

I'll tell you how it all happened. About two weeks ago at a Battery meeting, one of our juniors, Jack Keese, had a fit. At the time, everyone thought it was an epileptic fit, but we now have reason to believe it was caused by dope. Since that time, he has thrown at least four or five other fits and it usually falls my lot to help take care of him — my being "Fish Sergeant." When he has a fit, he gets red all over and his muscles twitch and jerk something awful. He foams at the mouth and his eyes are glassy. We have to take him up to his room — I personally never wanted to touch him but the Captain made me.

Well, tonight at a meeting, Keese got mad at Rex Grey,

a swell little guy, who is (or was) a junior in our Battery. They really swung some hard blows before they were separated. They settled down for a while, then they started arguing again. Rex jumped up saying he was going to the Captain. Keese followed within a few minutes. A little later we could hear them arguing upstairs. We heard a loud piercing yell choking into a gurgling noise which ended abruptly and then Keese came running down the stairs crying, "I didn't mean to do it! I didn't do it!" Then he had a fit and passed out cold.

Of course we all rushed upstairs to see what had happened. We expected Grey to be knocked out or something, but we were not prepared for the sight we saw. There on the floor lay poor little Rex with a cut about 4 or 5 inches long in his stomach. It was awful — a terrible gash with blood and his insides oozing out the cut. There was blood all over the room and a knife laying by his side. We recognized the knife as the one which the Captain had had stolen from his room a few days ago. One "Fish" claimed that he had seen Keese with it, but we had not believed him until now. The juniors immediately started hurrying us out of the room. They said for us to get to our "Holes" and stay there until they had conducted a thorough investigation. We didn't need any coaxing to get us to leave. They tried to get us to carry Keese to his room, but we would not touch him so they carried him up and locked him in.

Word has just been passed around that Keese has escaped and is running around like a madman, so we have barricaded the door with our dresser and trunks—just waiting for something to happen. I am holding a big iron pipe in my left hand as I write this note. If he comes around here, I'm going to hit him and I don't care if I put him out permanently. My roommate claims he saw him out the window running around in the courtyard. He wants a gun so he can shoot him. We are all scared stiff, I tell you, and I am writing this just to keep up my nerve. I am sure glad we are on the third floor. . . Just a minute, someone is knocking on the door and I have to help "My Old Lady" move the things out of the way . . . We are not taking any chances.

A couple of juniors came by to collect some money to send the Captain to Mexico. The evidence is too much against him with his knife beside the body, etc. Besides he is directly responsible for everything that happens in the Battery. For that matter, I am too, being "Fish Sergeant." That's why I am leaving out tomorrow morning early. So far the juniors have collected about thirty-three dollars.

Another knock at the door. . . One hour later—Boy, am

I relieved. I bet you could never guess what just walked into our room when we opened the door — the corpse. We nearly passed out sure enough this time until we discovered that he was very much alive. No kidding, I never thought I could be such a fool as to fall for such a trick as was pulled on the "Fish" of our Battery. Those upperclassmen surely had us scared. I should throw this letter away, but it really is too good to keep, so now I'll tell you how the whole thing was worked.

In accordance with a well laid plot, Keese had been throwing these fits for the benefit of the freshmen. He just now explained how he made them so realistic. Before each fit, he would hold his breath for a period of time which would cause him to turn very red from his waist up. He carried a hunk of tooth paste in his mouth which caused him to foam at the mouth. Things had gotten to the point that the "Fish" who cleaned up his room were afraid to be near him. He used to watch them with that glassy stare as they did the cleaning.

This morning, he and Grey purchased two live chickens in preparation for the mock fights. They cut the necks and caught all the blood in a glass. Next, they cut their livers out and other inner parts of the chickens were saved. These were placed on Grey's stomach to give the appearance of a deep gash. They poured the blood over the wound and the stage was completely set for thirty unsuspecting "Fish."

The Captain came around and gave us our money back and at the same time, he gave us a little talk. He told us we were in college now and for us not to believe everything we saw, much less everything we heard, and to always reason things out before jumping at conclusions. Then he left us to ponder over the events of the night.

I've decided not to come home after all. Throw this letter away.

Elmer

College Station, Texas

Oct. 17, 1939

Dear Joe:

Saturday afternoon, I had the very distasteful task of washing "Sully." A freshman came around while I was eating and told me to hurry back to the dorm and report to the Captain. I didn't know what was up, so I went back to the hall with many misgivings as to what the terrible dew heads had cooked up for us to do. Of course I expect any day to find that those foolish and erratic sophomores have laid a trap for me to stumble into!

The Captain told me I was to take a crew of "Fish" out to wash "Sully." The proper procedure, he said, was to dress myself and crew in old, dirty clothes and equip everyone with brooms, soap and water. This done, we marched off in the direction of the bronze statue of Lawrence Sullivan Ross, ex-President of the College, former Governor of Texas, and a former General in the Confederate Army. (You should see "Sully" with one of the tops of the lamps on his bald head. He looks like one of the Kaiser's henchmen!)

Some pea heads came out to see that the job was well done, or at least, they gave that excuse. Kibitzers!

We poured some buckets of water into the small flower bed around the statue and proceeded to wash "Sully." We paddled around a little bit, and then one of the damp noggins told me that if every one of the "Fish" in my detail didn't come out with mud all over them, there would be many a sad consequence and that the Captain wanted to see every "Fish" on top of the statue at some time or other.

That's when the crew got busy! Everybody started to swing his broom, trying to knock the other fellow off so he could get on top of the statue. It was a mad scramble for the top and after we had had a good enough battle to satisfy the bloodthirsty onlookers, we were allowed to march back to the hall.

The first thing we had to do when we got back to the dorm was to gather around a certain stoop and pray for rain. We did this, and suddenly when all the heads were bent down low, there came a rush of water that scared us into really yelling. That was the upperclassman's way of making us presentable, so we could enter the hall. Of course, it was all fun.

Later Saturday afternoon, we gathered around a radio in the hall to listen to the football game between the Aggies and Villanova at the Rose Festival in Tyler. As you know, Villanova had won about twenty-two games without a single defeat, and they were favorites to take the Aggies. When the game was over, it was a different story though. I heard from one of the boys on the team that just before the game, Jim Thomason asked the coach to let him make a speech. As Tomason had hardly said a word all season, everyone was surprised to see him get up to make a speech in the dressing room. But the coach told him to get it off his chest, so Jim said: "Boys, them damned Yankees shot my grandpa in the nose. Let's go get 'em!"

Maybe that is why the Aggies took them to the tune of 33 to 7. We have a great team this year. We should win the Southwestern championship without any trouble. The opposing teams just can't stop our line or our backfield, especially Kimbrough. With Thomason in front of him, he's a cinch! He's what they call a "ten second" man.

I have some problems to work in M. E. so I'll say "so-long" until later.

Regards,

Elmer

College Station, Texas,

Tuesday Night, Oct. 17, 1939

Dear Mom:

This job of "Fish Sergeant" is not all it is cracked up to be. I have been assigned every imaginable detail to perform; I have stopped fights, kept order at yell practice, assisted the Captain in keeping boys in line at formations; yet, I seem to get blamed for everything that happens! I have been called to the Captain's room about every night during the past week to explain how things happened. It's just like I told you before — that bunch of sophomores are jealous of me because I am able to ram them. Tomorrow I am supposed to help in drill. I have been studying my bull text very thoroughly as I must know all the movements if I am going to instruct the boys.

Thursday Morning.

I know I should have finished this letter sooner, but I just couldn't bring myself to write. I haven't felt like doing anything since yesterday. I sure hate to tell you, Mom, but I've been court-martialed and demoted to the ranks like the rest of the "Fish." It all started in drill yesterday. It seemed like everything I tried to explain to the boys was wrong, especially when the Captain came around. I was called into the Captain's room and told I would have to study harder, and as punishment, he ordered me to take a bunch of "Fish" out in the courtyard in front of the hall and yell: "Twelve more days until cush!" Of course, that wasn't so bad, but some upperclassmen started razzing us to yell louder. They were all hanging their heads out the second story windows, and made us line up facing them almost under the windows. Then when we were yelling our loudest, they bombarded us with seven chocolate pies which had been sneaked out of the mess hall that noon. I caught one right in the snozzle, and that was the straw that broke the camel's back! I have always been sensitive about the big nose, and having chocolate pie smeared all over it just sorta set off the fireworks.

I ordered the "Fish" to rush the upperclassmen; which we did. We had a free-for-all hand fight which lasted about fifteen minutes. Three senior officers were sent to the hospital as a result of my left—there would have been more if the Officer of the Day hadn't stopped the fight.

The officers of my Battery then held a special court and I was convicted of insubordination and striking an officer. That afternoon at mess formation, I was called out in front of the company and the Captain drew his sabre and cut the sergeant stripes from my sleeve and demoted me to the ranks. Well, Mom, even though I was still mad as a hornet, I couldn't help it when some tears rolled down my cheeks then, standing out there in front of the whole company with the thought in my heart that I'd failed to remember the duties of my office. I felt pretty much like a heel when I walked into the mess hall with the eyes of the whole company on me and showing their distrust and reproach. I feel a little better, tho', this morning. The Captain looked in my room this morning and told me to keep my chin up. Anyway, don't worry about me, Mom.

Love to all,
Elmer

College Station, Texas

Oct. 24, 1939

Dear Joe:

I want to tell you about my Fort Worth corps trip last weekend. I was really anxious to make this trip as it was our first official corps trip of the year. Like all the other Aggies, I cut classes the day before and left early. Our English Prof laughingly commented: "If the Colonel declared a one-way corps trip to hell, every Aggie would cut classes the day before so he could get an early start!"

I didn't have much money to make the trip on, so I hitch-hiked up there, arriving about 8:00 the night before the game. The Aggies avail themselves of all possible means of transportation when on a corps trip. Some boys ride the special, some ride buses, a few have been known to ride in airplanes, and there were a few who caught the freight train — and a much larger number hitch-hiked.

I failed to make any previous reservation, so I had quite a time finding a room. I finally managed to get one, but there really wasn't any use for I slept only about two winks the whole night. Even then I didn't get to sleep on the bed, for every time I came in, the bed was loaded with Aggies.

I had sent my name into the Blind Date Bureau which was arranging dates between the Aggies and the girls from TSCW. The next day we Aggies gathered at the downtown department store where we were to meet the girls from Denton. They had a public address system over which the girls' names and then the Aggie's names were announced. When they called my name and I saw my girl they had for me, my heart nearly stopped beating! My, she was ugly! Well, one look at her and I ducked out at the nearest exit and went back to the hotel.

We had to parade through the downtown section of the city before lunch. The streets were lined with spectators all along the way. You know how long 5,000 Aggies can make a parade. We finally were through and on our way to get something to eat when I ran into a friend of mine. He asked me if I had a date and I told him about my sad experience with the Date Bureau. He told me he had a cute date for me if I wanted one. It seems that he had promised his girl that he would get her four girl friends dates, but so far he had been able to recruit only three Aggies. I put up the excuse of no money, but he stopped me with the news that the girls already had tickets to the game and that I could go with him in his date's car. To top it off, he said that we were all going out to his girl's house after the game for a chicken dinner. How could a fellow turn down such an offer! He also said that since I was doing him the favor of going, he would pay my way to the dance that night. By that time I was beginning to get suspicious. I just couldn't imagine all this luck coming to me without there being something wrong with the girl in question! However, it didn't take much argument to convince me, and I decided to take the chance. We went out to his girl's house where everybody was to meet. As I walked up the front steps, I said: "Oh gosh, here is where I see the ugliest girl I ever saw in my life." I had a surprise in store for me, though, for the girl turned out to be a cute blond, and boy, was she swell!

We rushed out to the game to get a good seat — gee, there sure was a crowd. We won 20 to 6, but TCU gave us a scare when they made a touchdown in the first few minutes of the game. However, after that it was the Aggies' day, and the highlight of the game was when Conatser made a beautiful run from one end of the field to the other for a touchdown.

Boy, what blocking!

The fried chicken was delicious that night, the dance was really swell, and best of all, I got some swell elegant courting—all for the price of a package of Doublemint.

I left for school at one o'clock Sunday afternoon and arrived at Waco about 7:30. Midnight found me still in Waco with a bunch of Aggies, but we finally got a ride. I was really glad to see Prexy's Moon shining across the plains. I thought I'd give you the high spots, and hope for an early bull session in which to tell you the rest.

Your friend,

Elmer

College Station, Texas,
Oct. 30, 1939

Dear Joe:

Hi Joe—how did you like that game? I told you we had a real team—what do you think?

How did you like the yelling that the corps did? We think it's the greatest yell section in the world, but the fact that it is so good is due to some hard work at yell practice. Every night after supper, students gather in front of the "Y" steps. While waiting for the band to arrive, "Fish" from different companies and troops fight it out for the steps, for each "Fish" has been instructed to be in the front line. The band "Fish" are supposed to keep everybody off the steps, so there's lots of excitement. When the yell leaders appear, a big yell goes up, and the upperclassmen behind us yell "hump it!" This is the position with hands on legs just above the knees, head up, tail down, and upper body bent over. However, the "Spirit of Aggieland" is sung at the position of attention.

There are two yells which have a particular significance. "Lizzie" is yelled only when our team wins and "Taps" is yelled when we lose. We haven't had to yell "Taps" this year, and I sure hope we don't have to. Another thing that is unique about our yelling section is the way the corps sways during the second chorus of the "Aggie War Hymn."

We have a lot of good yells, and it's the duty of every freshman to learn each one. If he does not there comes a time when he's invited to the "Freshman-Sophomore Social Activities Meeting," or bleed meeting, and after that he's eager to learn the yells and songs backwards.

At the beginning of yell practice, the yell leaders make a speech or two. Sometimes, it's nothing more than the latest dirty joke or bawdy story, and sometimes, it's a heart to heart talk about the importance of the "Twelfth Man." Then of course we all try to yell louder than before. You know, Joe, psychology is a great factor in these talks. If we've just won a game , they tell us we'll win next time if we yell our hearts out, and I know that's what we do. One thing that amazed the cheer leaders of other schools is that the Aggie yell leaders do not use a megaphone. We have a system: the yell leaders call the name of the yell out loud enough for the fellows down close to hear, and they pass the name back to those behind them. It works like clockwork.

We sometimes have what is called midnight yell practice. After the freshmen have gone to bed, the sophomores come around and wake up us, hollering: "Midnight yell practice—yell, Freshmen!" We get up in our pajamas, put on our slippers, and grab anything we can to cover up with, and run out to where the band is marching. The band marches all over the campus with the freshmen following behind. We end up at the "Y" steps, and have a regular practice which is over about one o'clock. Midnight yell practices are held the night before a big game or sometimes to celebrate a victory.

After each home game, we go up to the "Y" steps and have a sort of informal yell practice. In this, all the cadets form around the "Y" steps and yell to celebrate winning the game.

At every game the freshmen have to stand up and yell the entire time, and if a "Fish" comes back to the hall afterwords without being hoarse, it's just too bad. It's the life tho', Joe, and I sure do like it. I'd like for you to be here sometimes for a yell practice.

Your friend,
Elmer

"Hump It!—Fish"

College Station, Texas

Nov. 5, 1939

Dear Bill:

First, I think I had better introduce myself as being Elmer's "Old Lady" and explain the purpose of this letter. Elmer has told me so much about you that I seem to know you already, and besides, I have a very particular reason for writing you this. I know you've wondered why you've had no answer to your last letter, which I note has been lying on the desk here unanswered for two weeks. Elmer said his mother told you about the "Fish Sergeant" incident, and that you wanted to know more about what happened, but I think it's up to me to tell you the whole story. You see, Bill, Elmer was sorta broken up about it at first, until he found out the whole thing was a joke and that he'd been taken for a ride by the upperclassmen in our organization. Of course, it was all in the best of fun with no harm meant, and I'm sure Elmer is about to become reconciled to the idea. Naturally, no one but me knows how he's really taken the whole thing for he came through in grand style as far as the boys could tell. When he found out it was a joke, he laughed loudest of all but just to show them he could really take it, he challenged all of the upperclassmen to a boxing duel. A lot of them took it up, and every afternoon and night last week, he went to the gym and boxed them one by one. You won't believe it Joe, but Elmer won over half of the fights and boy, was I glad. I had to go down and be his manager and it kept me pretty busy. It did me good to see the Captain of the outfit get up so slow after Elmer socked him with a heavy right, and all Elmer walked off with was one black eye and the admiration of every man in the outfit. They all got together in his room last night and gave him a feed, and you know, they looked mighty pleased to see Elmer's "Fish Sergeant" stripes hanging in an important place above our door.

I know you are wondering how they came to pick on Elmer when they chose the "Fish Sergeant." I really don't know why they chose him for this brief period of glory, but I guess they thought he didn't know the score. And too, you know that Elmer's looks are a perfect foil for that shifty boxing he does; he's tall and lean with a sort of sleepy look. Anyway, the big idea behind all this "Fish Sergeant" business is just to have some fun with a green. After the "Fish Sergeant" has received his commission, stripes, and all the honors conferred therewith he has certain duties to perform: to keep order in the ranks, quell fights within the outfit, and be an all around "order preserver." I guess they thought Elmer was a natural for the role of "Fish Sergeant," but the first fake fight the upperclassmen pulled gave a big surprise to everybody concerned. For Elmer knew how to handle them, and in fact was good!

Of course, at first we "Fish" thought the whole thing was on the level, but we finally caught on to the fact that they were taking Elmer for a ride. But you know I couldn't afford to say anything because I felt that a lot depended on how he came out of it. A lot of the upperclassmen got bruised black and blue as a result of some of the fake brawls they started, and when they found they were getting the worst of the whole deal, they decided it was high time they got together and impeached Elmer just to save their own skins. So they cooked up some phony charge against him, and with great pomp and ceremony, relieved him of his service stripes. They had to do it to save their own skins, for I could easily see that Elmer was holding his own and more in every peace making venture. So you see, he's really the better off for the whole thing. When a fellow is a senior, he is rated by the others according to how good a "Fish" he was. All the fellows like Elmer, and in fact, I'm just basking in the reflection of the limelight they've turned on him. Upperclassmen are always dropping by our room for a chat, and I heard Elmer's senior tell some fellows the other day that he was really proud of his freshman ! I'm sure glad I can tell you that Elmer came through it like a regular fellow.

Your friend, and Elmer's "Old Lady",

Jim

College Station, Texas

Nov. 6, 1939

Dear Joe:

It seems that I have done a lot of writing in your direction lately, but I always know that you have read the newspaper accounts and are waiting to hear my side of the story. Of course, on paper, the story loses some of the snap which you find in the regular bull sessions but somehow, it always makes a swell time seem more real to me if I can tell you about it. Some mighty yarns have been swapped between we two, but this trip to Arkansas was as unexpected as it was eventful and so I want to add it to our collection.

When we members of the Aggie Band learned that we were going to Arkansas to play for the football game between the Aggies and University of Arkansas in Fayetteville, we all were overjoyed. Most of us had never been to Arkansas so the trip promised to be something both new and exciting in the way of band trips. We were due to leave College Station at 6 o'clock Friday evening, and as might have been expected, a Norther blew in Friday morning, making it plenty cold. We gathered together everything we could wear because we expected it to be much colder up in Fayetteville than it was here, and we wanted to be prepared.

According to the old custom existing in the band, we freshmen loaded the instruments on the train, and everyone settled down to a long train ride. We got into Dallas that night at about 11 o'clock and by this time, most of the boys were in very high spirits; that is, those who hadn't fallen asleep. The conductor announced that we would stay in Dallas for forty-five minutes so everyone piled off the train and took over the Union Station.

That was the last stop of any consequence, so most of us went to sleep as soon as the train left Dallas. The next thing I remember is waking up next morning about 7 o'clock to find that we were riding through the hills of Eastern Oklahoma and were about one hour's ride from Arkansas.

Sack lunches were served on the train for breakfast and after we had eaten, we changed to our No. 1's. By that time we were in Fayetteville to witness the celebration. Pretty girls seemed to be unusually plentiful, so our first impression of Arkansas University was very favorable.

I didn't have much time to look at the girls, though, for we freshmen had to unload the instruments. We played in a parade which covered practically all of Fayetteville, uphill and downhill, and by the time the parade was over, I was plenty hungry. After eating dinner and exploring the business district for about an hour, we headed out to the stadium via the thumb route.

When we got to the University, it was quite a while before game time so we visited some of the fraternity and sorority houses which were scattered over the hilly campus. We were cordially received and enjoyed seeing how life in a co-ed school is lived. It looked pretty good for a change!

The game that afternoon was a real thrill, although the Aggies seemed to score whenever they chose. Their passing made me dizzy, and I see since that the newspapers called it "razzle-dazzle," which is a pretty descriptive word. As you know, Joe, we won 27-0. The weather had warmed up and everyone was feeling swell. There were only about three hundred Aggies at the game, but we made as much noise, if not more, than the whole Arkansas student body. Of course, we had more to yell about.

That night, Aggies were scattered all over Fayetteville. Some went to the big football dance at the gym. We didn't know any of the Arkansas girls but that didn't keep us from having a swell time. The Arkansas boys introduced us to all the girls they could. If one of us happened to be standing around watching, some Arkansas boy would come introduce himself. Then he would take us around and introduce us. Not all of the boys went to the dance. Some were standing around on street corners, waiting for something to pop up. A few went out to one or two of the honky-tonks, which they said were really worth the money. Some of the boys took over the instruments of the musicians and began to swing out on the "Aggie War Hymn," all in good fun.

Somehow, though, we all managed to get back to the train and, in a little while, we were Texas bound. Souvenirs ranged from red checked hillbilly caps to pearl studded sorority pins. I didn't rate a sorority pin, Joe, but I guess it's a good thing I didn't for I don't have time to write any more anyway, and that would call for another story. I just wanted to tell you about what a grand time I did have.

Your friend,
Elmer

College Station, Texas

Nov. 12, 1939

Dear Joe:

I must tell you of all the things that happened here Armistice Day. In keeping with the occasion and in honor of the fifty-two A&M men who died during the World War, our Cadet Colonel Woody Varner and his Staff placed a wreath on the Memorial at the old entrance at noon. After the sounding of the Assembly at the noon meal formation, the entire corps was brought to "Parade Rest" by each organization. After a brief pause during which announcements were made over the amplifier, the roster of A&M men who lost their lives in the services of their country in the World War was read. After each name was pronounced, a short roll was sounded by drummers detailed for that purpose. During the reading of the names of those fifty-two former Aggies who paid the supreme sacrifice, I said to myself: "God, bless America — the home of the free and the land of the brave, where our greatest battles are fought upon the gridiron!"

Then I thought of the countries of Europe, once again leaping at each others' throats like snarling wolves straining at a leash, waiting—yes, hopefully waiting for some imaginative excuse to sever the restraining thread of peace. You know, Joe, we are constantly reminded of the good fortune which is ours for just living in a peaceful nation. For instance, the other day while I was sitting in class, there broke into the peace of the moment the sound of an airplane. It was over our roof, but it was away almost as soon as it came, leaving the same peace as before. I guess I'm a funny guy, Joe, but I sorta said a prayer of thanks to God for the peace remaining—the quietude of a peaceful nation. And then I thought of the importance of our men—yes, the Texas Aggies, and every thinking youth of the land, in leading the way toward an everlasting peace.

Here's what I think, Joe. First, we must have peace within ourselves. How can we have peace within ourselves, for it is in vain to seek it from an outward source. I think Rochefoucauld said that, didn't he? I like the idea which Patrick set forth when he said:

"The more quietly and peacefully we all get on, the better — the better for ourselves — the better for our neighbors. In nine cases out of ten, the wisest policy is, if a man cheats you, quit dealing with him; if he is abusive, quit his company; if he slanders you, take care to live so that nobody will believe him no matter who he is, or how he misuses you, the easiest way is generally to let him alone; for there is

nothing better than this cool, calm, quiet way of dealing with the wrongs we meet with. Peace is the proper result of the Christian temper. It is the great kindness which our religion doth us that it brings us to settledness of mind, and a consistency within ourselves."

When the last name was read, "Attention" was sounded, and the Corps was brought to this position by organization. Then over the amplifier, the strains of "Silver Taps" floated out over the campus. At the first note of Taps, all uniformed cadets in rank or out of ranks gave the salute and remained at salute until the last note drifted out over the stillness of the hour. We were paying our highest tribute to the Aggies who gave their lives for our country. I thought back to my first week in school when I had to count the stars in the flag hanging in the Academic Building. I counted fifty-two gold stars in the center commemorating the dead, and 1,948 others honoring the men who came back. Just think of it, Joe, two thousand Aggies served in the Army, Navy and Marine Corps during the war — more officers were furnished by A&M than by any other college in the United States. It was a thoughtful Aggie corps which marched into the mess halls a few minutes later.

I have some more to tell you about the events of Armistice Day, including the accounts of the game but I'll have to wait until tomorrow to write it. You may not have anticipated receiving a letter in serial form, but I'm afraid that's what you'll get this time.

Your friend,

Elmer

College Station, Texas

November. 13, 1939

Joe:

Here I am again!

Now for an account of the game. I know you said you wouldn't find it possible to hear the game over the radio, but I am sure you have read about the final score. We won 6 to 2 and if you think that wasn't a close margin, you are completely wrong! I was scared!

As you know, SMU had won every game except two, tying with Oklahoma and losing to Notre Dame by the slim score of 19 to 20, so the eyes of the nation's football followers were once more turned toward the Southwest Conference for the top game of the nation. We had the slight advantage playing the Mustangs in our own backyard as we had the famous "Twelfth Man" out in full force. The special Armistice edition of THE BATTALION carried a poem by Mr. J.W. Amyx, which I think tells how we felt before the game. I've copied it for you, below:

> What's this son?
> You wonder why you have to stand
> And yell,
> Why you have to sing like hell,
>
> Listen, son, listen —
> Hear the sound of marching feet;
> Hear the footfalls echoing through
> the street.
>
> Listen youngster, listen —
> It's those Mustangs you gotta beat;
> I'll tell you now it's quite a feat.
>
> Wait, don't run, wait son —
> If you'll fight, it can be done,
> Fight hard and game is won.

Listen, youngster, listen—
Hear that twelfth man yell—
Makes you wanna fight like hell.

Wait, son, wait—

Here an ex's last word—
That's the best yellin' I ever heard.

Listen, youngster, listen—
It's for the team they yell,
The team that fights like hell.

Bill Stern, the ace sports commentator for the National Broadcasting Company, gave a play-by-play description of the game over a coast-to-coast network. And boy was it exciting to watch! We were leading 6 to 2, the result of a touchdown for the Aggies and a blocked punt by the Mustangs. In the closing minutes of the game, SMU unleashed an aerial attack that advanced the ball within the very shadow of our goal. With only seconds remaining, they completed beautiful passes in the dampest weather we've had in many moons. The final whistle blew just as an Aggie and a Mustang leaped into the air for the pass that would spell victory or defeat, for our team. It seemed the ball was in the air for an eternity, leaving the Aggies with another great victory. The corps was so excited, we nearly forgot to give the victory yell, "Lizzie."

LIZZIE

(First three rahs slow)

Rah! Rah! Rah!

Is my hat on straight?

Lend me your powder rag,

Sweet cherry phosphate!

1! 2! 3!

Team!

You must think my pen is well-oiled tonight, but there's one thing more to tell you about in connection with the happenings on Armistice Day. Looks like I'm going to get this letter finished in one installment for it won't take so much time to tell you about the dance after the game. You see, after each home game, there is a football dance staged in Sbisa Hall. Lots of fun! This particular dance was probably the most unique one of the season. Music was furnished by Fahy Godfrey of South Texas fame and Tommy Littlejohn of Aggieland. The orchestras were located at each end of the hall

They alternated playing at thirty minute intervals. Sbisa Hall is the largest dining hall under one roof in the world, and what I mean it was packed from orchestra to orchestra! Tommy Littlejohn introduced the new song for which we had been waiting so long—"I'd Rather Be a Texas Aggie." It was written by his brother, Jack—a good Aggie. Be sure to buy a copy when it is published for it is really good. It goes something like this:

I'd rather be a Texas Aggie, a mean so and so

Than be from any other school and rolling in dough;

I'd rather be out on the highway a thumbin' a ride

Than have a Miss Greta Garbo for my blushing bride

For I'm true to the colors of maroon and white,

If they win or lose—or if they're wrong or right;

But if they lose, old pal—you'll always hear me say—

Let's go to Ed's and drink our cares away. I'd rather be out on

a corps trip, No dime to my name.

Than to have my picture painted in the hall of fame;

Just rather be a plain old Aggie, no shirt or no tie—

I'll always be an Aggie 'til the day I die.

So much for that, and I think I'd better put an end to this epistle before I run the postage up to nine cents instead of six. How about a long letter in return for this one? You know, "My Old Lady" said one would think you and I were two old maids swapping experiences, the way we write one another. But he just hasn't known me long enough to know that you and I went through fighting Beeno, the bully and soundly trounced Wilbur, the sissy, when we were in grammar school for no other reason than that we liked to do things together!

So long,
Elmer

College Station, TX

Nov. 28, 1939

Dear Homer August:

I received your most welcome letter several days ago and I had planned to write sooner, but I have been so busy I didn't have time.

This school is a swell place, but it isn't a bed of roses for a lowly "Fish." The upperclassmen make us work like hardy pioneers, believing that hard work and no play make a good . I believe the hardest task we have is cleaning up their rooms. I clean up for two pee-heads, and what I mean, they are terrible. One of them was a low-life-day-dodger last year but he doesn't give me much trouble. You should see the other one, because if you have never seen a human chimpanzee, you've missed something! He really looks tough and he certainly doesn't let his looks deceive you — he tries to be as tough as he looks, and so he gives me plenty of trouble. But then, that's the life here.

Since you are planning on coming up here next year, maybe I'd better start telling you some of the things you can expect to take place when you get to A&M. Just now I don't have time to enumerate all of the things that are sure to happen to you, but I can tell you about one tiresome duty which every "Fish" has to contend with. And that's the job of cleaning up an upperclassman's room. I'll give you the routine:

When you first enter the room, a mass of dirty clothes, two desks of unstacked books, and a floor covered with dirt greets the eye. The books have to be picked up, clothes hung in the closets, and the windows opened so that a good draft is formed through the room. The draft will help carry the dust out as you sweep. If the upperclassman's shoes are lined up neatly under the bed, it's possible to get out of sweeping that particular spot for two and three days.

Now you must clean the desks. All of the books must be placed neatly on the shelves; all pencils, pipes, letters, and money, if any, all must be placed in respective drawers. With a dirty towel, the top of the desk must be polished and the lamp dusted. (I broke two reflectors trying to dust table lamps with one hand! I'll tell you what I learned — use two hands).

The lavatory must be washed before the upperclassman gets up, but it's better to wait until his hair has been combed and oiled before you attempt to straighten out the chest of drawers. Then to the bed, which must be made up neatly. The covers usually look as if they'd been hard hit by a cyclone, but

a good system of re-spreading the cover takes up less time than trying to make the bed over entirely.

After the senior has finished with the lavatory, it's time to clean the mirror. I usually do this with a tissue. Then if everything appears to be in a straightened condition, it's time to ask for permission to leave. Of course on laundry day, all the dirty clothes have to be gathered up, and then the clean laundry placed in its place. Then on sunny Sunday afternoons, The bedding has to be beaten and sunned, and all that calls for a real clean-up job for the room.

I think the duty of room cleaning will probably be your most tiresome duty. Maybe you'd better get in practice by helping your mother clean house. However, after a few house cleanings, you may decide you would prefer to attend some other college. Still, I think you'd get to like it here and after your "Fish" year, it's all smooth sailing. We really don't do enough to hurt us any, and I think I can keep step with all that host of freshmen who have gone before me.

Your friend,
Elmer

P.S. I forgot to mention that we "Fish" have to go to the post office after every meal for our upperclassmen. Being lowly "Fish," we are not allowed to walk on sidewalks. We have to walk in the streets, rain or shine.

It always burns the upperclassmen up when I get a couple of letters and they don't get any. And if I get one addressed in feminine scrawl, then that's twice as bad, and they give me a little extra duty just to even up the score. But I like to hear from home so you'd better write me again soon.

E.H.

College Station, Texas

Dec. 4, 1939

Dear Tom:

I know you have a good team up there at the University of Richmond, but have you heard about the Texas Aggies? If you have read the papers, you will notice that the Associated Press rates the Aggies as the Number One team of the nation. I want to tell you about our Thanksgiving game with the University. The Number One team of the nation really had what it takes that day.

In keeping with an Aggie tradition, we "Fish" built an immense bonfire to be burned the night before the game. Picture 2,000 freshmen building a four story bonfire. The preparations began with all the sophs of various organizations having special bleed meeting at which the "Fish" were told how to build a bonfire, and where to get the wood. The railroad company promised to give us several car loads of crossties if we would not bother the rest of the property. It seems that in the past, some unthinking Aggie had torn up a spur of track in order to please a demanding sophomore. Every available piece of wood for miles around was piled on the stack. Axes, saws, and trucks aided the ambitious "Fish". Even trees were uprooted. Bridges, sign posts, telephone poles, out houses, shacks — everything in sight was confiscated! We came to one old rambled shack which we thought was empty, so under cover of night we proceeded to tear it down.

After demolishing several rooms, we discovered that an old man was living in one of the rooms. We didn't disturb his slumber, but the next morning found him complaining to the College Officials. We're still paying for the damage. However, after that, the Bull started checking up on material that went into the building of the bonfire. The boys would just bring the wood to the edge of the drill field and leave it until the Bull left. Then sometime the Sarg was watching, so several of the "Fish" would have to get him off and talk while the other put any suspicious looking pieces of the wood on the stack. We swiped several three-holers from North Gate and hid them in the new dorm area, planning to put them on at the last minute. The owner raised so much devilment they had to be carried back.

After the first two days the "Fish" had to keep guard day and night to keep the tea sippers from Texas off the grounds. Some of them always try to set it off before time. The guard details were worked out by companies. Each outfit would take watch for twenty-four hour periods, and each guard consisted of forty to fifty boys. They had a siren for an alarm, and we usually had one or two false alarms each night. Within thirty seconds after an alarm was sounded, the frill field would be swarming with Aggies in their pajamas, loaded down with clubs, buckets of water, or anything handy to use in a free for all fight. Crossties formed a block all around the bonfire to prevent cars driving near it.

One year a group of Texas students drove down to set off the bonfire early, only to be met by the Army. Their new car was somewhat damaged, and one of the boys shaken up considerably.

The night for firing the bonfire finally arrived and the frizzling rain which fell all day could not dampen our spirits. We soaked the wood with kerosene and started the fire as soon as it was dark. The frill field was lined with cars and Aggies, and Aggie boosters were packed around in a circle. The yell leaders lead the Aggies yells from a specially constructed platform equipped with an amplifier. It was lots of fun in spite of the rain.

The next day was equally as exciting. A Thanksgiving dinner of turkey and all the trimmings put us in the right mood for a wonderful time. According to the signs hung around the mess hall we were due to a treat of "Cranberries and "Davie's Mountain Oysters". Every week before an important game, the "Fish" of various organizations paint large signs about three feet by ten, and hang them at all available places around the mess hall, Academic building, and even in the trees.

Just before the game started, several University of Texas students distributed some soil over the playing field. This dirt was brought from their own gridiron so that the Steers could play on their own soil— (a crazy idea!). Anyway, its significance was determined by the final score.

The first half ended with the score 0-0. Between the halves, Coach Norton stepped into his team's dressing room and said: "Boys, let's take them now!" That was the only thing he said—he just turned on his heels, and left it up to the team. The Steers kicked off to the Aggies and the first play was the old sleeper play which worked perfectly. "Bama" Smith stood near the sidelines and took a 46 yard pass which set the stage for the first touchdown. The Longhorns' resistance seemed to weaken after that. The Aggies scored twice more, and the game ended 20-0. That game gave the Aggies ten wins with no defeats for a perfect season. How is that for a football team! Watch us in one of the bowl games. The Aggies placed two men on most all of the All-American teams. They were John Kimbrough at full-back and Joe Boyd at tackle. Listen in when Kate Smith presents the specially designed and engraved 17-jewel Bulova wrist watches to the members of her All-American team.

The next time you are around at 2230 Park Avenue, give my regards to Barbara and Janie.

Well, I must do some studying.

Write me,

Elmer

College Station, Texas

Dec. 5, 1939

Dear Joe:

I suppose you noticed in the papers where A&M And the University of Tennessee were offered $80,000.00 each if they would play in the Cotton Bowl on New Year's Day. As you know, Tennessee is expecting a bid to the Rose Bowl and will not give a definite answer. I don't know whether they are afraid of the Aggies or not, but we certainly are not afraid of them and to be honest, we are anxious to play them at Dallas so that the Texas people will have a chance to see their favorite team in action. The team is going to vote today to decide whether to play in the Cotton Bowl or the Sugar Bowl at New Orleans.

Wednesday Morning.

Last night, the team voted to play Tulane in the Sugar Bowl. Tulane is rated as the number two team in the Nation. Tennessee refused to make a decision on the Cotton Bowl game as they are waiting for an invitation to the Rose Bowl. I guess they'll get it, too, because the West Coast teams are afraid of the Aggies after our victory over Santa Clara 7-3.

The team figured the best move would be to accept the Sugar Bowl invitation, so we're going to get to go to New Orleans.

Grantland Rice, ace sports writer, wired the Sugar bowl Officials the following message:

Herb Benson.

President, Sugar Bowl.

Congratulations on getting Tulane and Texas A&M for the Sugar Bowl game. Should be a knockout between two of the strongest bowl teams for many years. Will be glad to help in any way.

Regards,

Grantland Rice

Now when Grantland Rice says two teams are strong, they must be for he has been tops among sports writers of the nation for many years.

I can hardly wait for the holidays to come. How would you like to hitch-hike down to New Orleans with me? You could wear an Aggie uniform and we won't have any trouble, I am sure.

Regards, Elmer

College Station, Texas

Dec. 18, 1939

Dear Bill:

I know you have been interested in attending A&M. Next fall after you complete high school I know you said you wanted to study Agriculture, and if you come to this college, you will come to the school which boasts of the largest enrollment in the School of Agriculture in the United States. A&M has produced some outstanding men in the field of Animal Husbandry, and I think it is a great thing for us too, since records show that Texas is the outstanding livestock state in the nation.

For your information, I am enclosing a clipping taken from **The Battalion** concerning a report made by Mr. D. W. Williams, Head of Animal Husbandry Department of A&M, to Mr. E. J. Kyle, Dean of the School of Agriculture.

Records From Chicago Prove Texas To Be Outstanding Livestock State

COLLEGE STATION, DEC. 18. — D. W. Williams, Head of Animal Husbandry Department at Texas A&M, recently turned in a report to Dean E. J. Kyle listing some accomplishments of Texans in the animal industry field this year.

Many readers have seen the individual items in the newspapers, but collected in one report they make Texas the standout state in the nation.

Here is Mr. Williams' letter to Dean Kyle:

Dear Dean Kyle:

Several things happened during the recent International Livestock Exposition at Chicago that I think would interest you. I thought I would call your attention to some of these items as it is possible that you might have overlooked them in the newspaper accounts.

The grand champion steer of the show was a Hereford shown by Mayfield Kothmann of Mason, Texas. The reserve grand champion was also a Hereford, shown by Jack Baker of Bluffdale, Texas. This is the first time that Texas ever won both the grand champion and the reserve grand championship.

The reserve grand champion bull and grand champion Hereford cow both were shown by Silver Creek farm of Fort Worth. This farm is managed by Jack Turner, a graduate of the college and former member of our judging team.

The 4-H Club livestock judging team won first place for the second consecutive year. The team this year was coached by Henry Kothmann, who was also formerly a member of one of our livestock judging teams and is a graduate of the college. The team last year was coached by H. A. Fitzhugh, himself also a judging team member and graduate of the college.

The college livestock judging team stood fourth among the twenty-nine teams competing. Our meats judging team stood sixth, with fifteen colleges competing.

The Animal Husbandry Department showed one Aberdeen-Angus heifer, bred here at the college. This heifer won her class, was reserves junior champion, and sold for $2,000, which is the highest price ever received for a single animal by this college. So far as I know, this was the highest priced female sold at the Exposition.

Very truly yours,

D. W. Williams, Head of Department.

I thought you would be very interested in this information, since you are so anxious to go to the best and most economical agricultural school.

The best of the season's greetings to you and your mother.

Your friend, Elmer

College Station, Texas

Dec. 19, 1939

Dear Mom:

The Christmas spirit has hit Aggieland! The various clubs, organizations, etc., have been having Christmas parties which have been given by the freshmen for the upperclassmen. The highlights of the program held in Guion Hall Sunday afternoon. The Christmas carolers, the Aggie Glee Club and the Aggie concert band were featured on the program at Guion Hall. For the past two weeks, we "Fish" have been singing Christmas carols every night just before "Taps." The freshmen from each outfit gather in front of their respective dormitories and sing such old favorites as "Jingle Bells," "Silent Night," "Adeste Fideles," and others. We "Fish" in the band take this fine old tradition very seriously and sing the best we can. We've been forming a long line and walking around the new dormitory area singing the carols as one of the boy's plays an accordion.

Well, Mom, I'll be leaving here Wednesday afternoon — so keep the home fires burning until late that night. However, you'd better not wait up for me as I may not get home until

Thursday morning. I sure will be glad to get my feet under Mom's table once more!

I'm sure excited over the prospects of getting to go to New Orleans for the game. That's going to be about the best Christmas present you and Dad have ever given me.

Love,

Elmer

College Station, Texas

Dec. 19, 1939

Dear John:

We have just completed a full week here and I'm ready to go home tomorrow for the holidays. My Battery had its Christmas party last night, which topped off the past week of excitement.

About Monday a week ago, the "Fish" began bringing in the decorations, such as holly wreaths, etc. into the hall. We also wrote letters to Santa Claus, asking for nothing for ourselves but only presents for the upperclassmen. We didn't ask for anything useful—just silly things that "float out" the guys. All the letters were posted on our doors so everyone passing by could read them and laugh at the upperclassmen.

We took up a collection of about 35 cents each from all the "Fish" for refreshments and had our six gallon meeting at which there were no upperclassmen present. The Santa Claus we elected was a big fellow, jovial and boisterous. The idea of the Santa Claus is for a fellow to give out the presents and act as a general master of ceremonies. If the upperclassmen find out who Santa Claus is, the tradition is that they kidnap him and leave him on some lonely country road a long way from "no place" just before the party. We thought our selection was so obvious, that we managed to always have several of our toughest freshmen on hand to see that our genial merry man wasn't stolen from us on the eve of the party. I guess our selection was too obvious to be noticed, for they didn't know whom to kidnap.

For refreshments, we bought some fruit, cookies, and fruit juice plus cigars to keep the upperclassmen in good humor between acts.

At a wide space in the hall, we strung a wire across and put up a makeshift curtain. In the far corner of our stage, we had a Christmas tree decorated artistically with electric lights and Scott's tissue. Gifts for every upperclassman were placed around the bottom of the tree.

We freshmen got together the night of the party — or that is, just before the party, and caught a rather unpopular sophomore as he came up the hall. We slammed him in a car and took him out on a little road and left him. We really had meant to take most of his clothes off, but got to feeling sorry for him so we just left him on the side of the road in a presentable fashion.

We had hardly passed out the cigars and started the program when in came our stranded sophomore. He didn't take the episode very gracefully, but the rest of the upperclassmen overrode him in the jollity of the occasion, so he muttered his curses in his beard the rest of the evening.

For the program we had a quartet which lasted long enough to sing two songs. Then a wrestling match to end all wrestling matches. It was a burlesque of a faked rough and ready put on brawl. The two fellows, one little and the other one big, did it so cleverly that it brought down the house with cheers. The big fellow, to all appearances, nearly murdered the little one until the little guy asked for time out for his slide rule. He made a few rapid calculations, smiled knowingly and went to work on the big fellow. We carried the big fellow off the stage.

One of our acts was a mock court between St. Peter and the Devil. I was dressed as the Devil — my hair was rumpled all over my head and my face painted red. I wore red tights and an orange sweat shirt. We tried all the sophomores. Some were found so mean and "onery" that neither the Devil nor St. Peter wanted them. These were sent back to the "Fish" who took care of them in the proper manner. We couldn't decide which one would be forced to accept some of the pee-heads, so we shot craps to decide the unlucky one. I almost lost my pants one time, so I asked the Captain for his shoulder ornaments to pin them up. He was very embarrassed when the fellows all laughed.

We pulled the curtains then pulled off Santa Claus' toilet paper beard, and made him up to take the part of Little Nell in our Fish Art Players' interpretation of "Little Nell." It was the hit of the party. Little Nell played his part with tenderness and emotion. It was a great scene, Tom True, the valiant Texas Aggie, returned in time to save the homestead and Little Nell's honor with the money he won betting on the A&M football team.

Incidentally, "Little Nell" was played by the largest in our company and Tom True was the most emaciated.

Some of the most common presents were baby assortments, small dolls, packs, sink stoppers, mouse traps, soap, small toys, silk panties, sanitary pads, brassieres, some chicken feathers, and other small articles. The sophomore chosen by the "Fish" as being the most "chicken" was presented with a neatly and attractively wrapped box of debris from the Cavalry stables.

After the presents were distributed, refreshments were served and the party drew to a close with best wishes all around. The upperclassmen gave three cheers for the freshmen, and we "Fish" felt highly rewarded for our efforts.

Well, John, I guess I'll be seeing you in a few days. I'll only be home a few days but we should be able to get the old gang together for a good time while I'm home. Sure wish you and Joe would decide to head out to New Orleans with me for the Sugar Bowl game. I know it's going to be keen fun.

     Your friend,

     Elmer

College Station, Texas

Jan. 8, 1940

Dear Joe:

Do you remember my promise to write and tell you about the Sugar Bowl game and New Orleans? Well, this is the first chance I've had, so here goes. I even kept a little log book so I could make notes on things as they happened, and that way, I haven't forgotten anything.

Well, Mother let Jack and me (you knew Jack went along, didn't you?) out on the highway at 1:15 p.m., December 30. At exactly 1:30 we caught a ride with a Mr. and Mrs. Brittain, who took us all the way to Baton Rouge. The only stop was made at Sulphur, where we bought the Brittains coffee and hamburgers. It was about 7 o'clock when we crossed the Mississippi, and at 7:30, we left the Brittains in Baton Rouge. The most impressive thing about Louisiana so far was their coffee—it was awful!

We ate supper and cleaned up a bit, and were ready to leave Baton Rouge at eight o'clock. The people were as nice as could be; friendly, and helpful in every way possible.

It was about nine o'clock when we caught a ride to New Orleans, arriving there at 10:30. A drunk picked us up and decided to show us the town. We saw a lot of New Orleans, for he took us everywhere he could possibly think of, which was a lot, considering his "stewed" condition. He was overcome by our uniforms and manners, and simply couldn't get over the way we said "Yes Sir" and "No Sir," and stuff like that. He said he was going to send his son to A&M. He talked of taking us home with him for the night, but decided his wife might not like it since some of her relatives were already there.

"This town is wonderful! All the stores on Canal Street have large signs on them. One has a sign three stories high which says 'Welcome, Texas Aggies.' You can't imagine how wonderful everything is unless you've been here at New Years. All the Christmas decorations are still up — lights, trees, and big candles on all of the street lights. And above everything that friendly spirit seems to be everywhere! We had no rooms or any place to stay as everything was reserved, so we had to stay in some lobby. There were plenty of Aggies doing the same thing, though, so we didn't feel out of place."

The above paragraph was taken directly out of our log book for I was afraid re-writing would take away the feeling of enthusiasm which I am sure you'll find in the words just as they were jotted down.

After looking over the city for awhile, we checked our

bags at the Roosevelt Hotel and washed up. Then we started out to make every joint in town. Joe, you know I don't drink but this time, the temptation was too great! Everyone was drinking, and trying to get me to; so, it goes without saying that the holiday spirit made me give in. We went to the Jung Cocktail Bar, Flynn's and a number of other places. At the St. Charles Bar, we met Hazel from Houston, who bought us a Tom Collins or two.

You should have seen your pal — the mirrored ceiling reflected this Texas Aggie with one foot propped on the proverbial brass rod, wedged in between a tipsy blond and some prosperous fellow who insisted on paying for the drinks. Ramus Gin Fizz, Whiskey Sour, Tom Collins, and other mixed drinks whose names were different but with the same general effect! And Planters Punch, topped with a red cherry which, strange as it may seem, brought a moment of pathos as I thought of that day when you and I enacted one of the highlights of George Washington's boyhood and caught a paddle on the seat of our pants!

The walls of the St. Charles Bar were lined with paintings of lovely nude women; or that is dressed in much too long and much too flowing tresses which captured the imagination. It was a sight to behold! Men lined these walls, standing shoulder to shoulder, and from the crowd rose laughter and smoke and a thickening aroma of scotch and bourbon, but an adventurous spirit drove us back into Canal Street.

About 2:30, we went back to the Roosevelt. Ozzie Nelson was playing in the Hawaiian Blue Room. His vocalist, Rose Ann Stevens, wanted tickets to the game so we got some for her, and to return the favor, she got us into the blue room. It was swell!

After the dance, we made our bed; or that is, there were several Aggies about so we pulled a bunch of chairs together as a barricade and went to sleep on the floor about 3:30 a.m. "My Old Lady" came into the lobby and woke me up about six o'clock the next morning. He had his car, so we went down to meet the train from College Station.

While we were waiting for the train, a man asked Jack to put his bags off the train. Jack did it out of politeness, and the man tipped him $5.00. We met the special and the band, and then rode all over town. Finally, we went down to the dock and went aboard a battleship. We were given a lot of privileges because we were in the Army. We made friends with a bunch of young sailors who promised to meet us later and show us the town.

When we got back to town, we found two tickets on the 40-yard line. They were laying on the street with no means of identification anywhere around. We sold them for $11.00. That was the start! We started scalping on tickets and made plenty of money.

Joe, remember that was the night Josephine was to sing on the radio. Well, we caught a ride in a car with a radio so we could listen to her, and rode as far as the man would take us. The program was only half over when we got out, so we walked to the nearest house, knocked on the door, and asked if we might listen to the radio. They said, "Sure;" so we went and listened to her. When "Jo" won the contest, we all nearly tore the house down! There was a beautiful blond living there who is a Sophie Newcombe. We asked her for a date, but she had one, so we thanked the family profusely and left. When we got to town we sent some flowers.

That night was even more hectic than the one before. We made every place that we hadn't made. Most of the "honkytonks" and dives, characteristic of old New Orleans are within three or four blocks of Canal Street on the French side. About 9:30, we branched off of Canal Street and began making these. With our uniforms, we did not lack attention. I walked into a dive and a fairly drunk female hung onto me. Occurrences such as this were not infrequent, but we didn't run into any real trouble. We walked by a dark, secluded doorway, and noticed an attractive young woman standing just outside. She beckoned us to enter, so we went in to see what would happen. Although we had no intention of making a purchase, we talked her down from two dollars to a dollar and a half, and then made some excuse to leave.

We found our way back to Canal Street and to the hotel. It was then about 3:15 o'clock, so we decided to find a place to sleep. All the space in the lobby was taken, except under the big Christmas tree, so we crawled under and tried to sleep. We didn't get much sleep though, for everyone was constantly waking us to wish us a Happy New Year. So after a series of naps, we go up about seven and some kind of gentleman bought our breakfast.

We bought and sold tickets all morning until game time. Made some more money.

We got to the stadium about noon, to find it already half-packed. We were there in time to see the Aggie team come into the stadium from Biloxi, and believe me, they looked like champions! However, there were thousands of people there that day who had to be shown!

Before the game, the New Orleans Legion Band, led by two curvaceous majorettes, and the Orange High Bengal Guards paraded the length of the field several times. Aerial bombs broke over the stadium, releasing tiny white parachutes which carried pennants of A&M. and Tulane, as well as the American flag, to lend a carnival air to the greatest spectacle I've ever witnessed.

Joe, you probably heard the description of the game over the radio. In fact, I'm sure you wouldn't miss it. Well, everything was just as the announcer said, only more so. There was something in the air when Kimbrough and Boyd walked out onto the field as co-captains of the day. We all sorta sat back and relaxed during the first quarter because the marching Aggies took possession of the field. By substituting a new team, Tulane made plenty of ground through quick opening plays and before we knew it, the game was in the third quarter and the score was tied. I thought my heart was down as low as it could get, but when a fumble gave the Green Wave the ball on the Aggie 39, I was sunk! In the beginning of the last period, Tulane snatched their second touchdown, and there weren't many dry eyes when Herbie Smith blocked the try for the point, for we knew that the fighting Texas Aggies could still turn the tide! And that's where Jarring Jawn and our championship team took charge to make a neat finish. A lateral to John gave us the tying score, and when Cotton Price kicked that sweet extra point, we went wild! All I knew for the next moments was the pounding of hands on shoulders and the din of cheering Aggies. In fact, the whole crowd cheered unreservedly, for they knew champions when they saw them!

Our team then made another bid for one more score, but the final gun found them just short of the Greenies goal. Thus, the game ended 14 to 13, for the crowning moment of a day, long to be remembered. Joe, I don't think there's ever been anything like it since the beginning of Aggieland, and I was proud to be an Aggie!

After the game, we went back to town, and the streets were lined with Aggie boosters who walked arm in arm, singing the "Aggie War Hymn" or shouting their praises. "Kimbrough" was the newsboy's cry! Wherever we turned, it was "The Aggies!" This was the sight we hated to leave, but we had to catch the seven o'clock train to Houston. Anyway, we were dead tired and wanted to sleep. It was a marvelous trip, we saw everything, did everything, and ended up with $11.00 more than we had to start with. We had such a swell time, I wish it was all to do over again and that you might be there to do it with us.

Sincerely your friend,
Elmer

College Station, Texas

Jan. 15, 1940

Dear Tom:

The past few days have been really busy ones for me. During the weekend, the freshmen class held its annual ball. It was a big success in every respect. Financially, it was the most successful dance ever given by freshmen at A&M. As for the enjoyment, I am sure it was the best that we'll have this year.

As you know, there is a shortage of girls here at school, and for an affair such as this one, girls are brought in from all parts of Texas and surrounding states. They come down in bus loads from TSCW at Denton. It is a known fact that the freshmen rate the best looking girls, and considering the girls on campus last weekend, I think we're maintaining our reputation pretty well. There were more gorgeous brunettes, glamorous blonds and curvaceous red heads than ever before seen at one gathering. Even so, there weren't enough girls to go around.

Because there was a shortage of girls, there was much bird dogging going on, especially on the part of the seniors who were guests of the freshman class at the freshman ball.

The seniors tried to dazzle the girls with their boots and trappings. At this time of the year the A&M campus is besieged by startling numbers of a peculiar species of bird dog. They are known by the scientific name "male dogietus de rotientfemilas," which when translated means the pals turn rat and get the girl.

Of course you can guess I had a date by the way I criticize the bird dogs. It was a lot of trouble keeping up with my date because she was a swell dancer and from the first dance to the last, she was in demand by many — too many. Once I had to cut in six times during a single number before I got to take over four steps. Because there was a shortage of girls, there was much bird dogging going on, especially on the part of the seniors who were guests of the class at the ball.

Since I didn't have much luck getting to dance with her, I suggested we leave early. (Guess my real reason!) The moon and stars made the evening complete as we two sat there waiting for the other to say something. Since I had known her only a short time, I was a little slow in getting started. But I finally got my arm around her waist and this made the rest of the night heaven! As our lips touched and my arms pulled her closer, it seemed as if the love bug had bitten me with a bang. We looked into each other's eyes, and I just knew she was the only one — so, I told her I loved her.

Tom, I made one little mistake and I want to warn you so you'll be careful. When I said: "Darling, I love you so," she let go a blow that landed on the side of my face! I still have the print of her hand on the side of my face. She called me a liar, said I had been out with her roommate the night before, and that I was just another Aggie! Well, that's women for you — they're never satisfied. I'm off women for life.

Your friend,

Elmer

College Station, Texas

Jan. 17, 1940

Dear Mr. Collins:

Knowing that you are interested in some facts about A&M for a book that you are planning to write, I am writing to tell you something about the traditions of Aggieland. The Texas Agricultural and Mechanical College is one of the largest all-male Land Grant colleges in the country.

Tradition is one of the most cherished possessions of the Aggies. A&M is not like most all-male colleges. Here we have no strict administrative body, no police to speak of, no elders living with us in dormitories, or any of the other things such as rules and regulations. Why? Because these things are taken care of by tradition.

One of the first things a new student on the campus learns is that there is a certain "handle" -FISH- that must be attached to his name every time he meets someone. And this leads to another tradition. The most important duty of a freshman is to meet every man in his organization and not only to know the name of each, but also the hometown and the course which he is taking.

Why is this the most important duty? First, because it will help him to keep from getting homesick and second, because these contacts will prove valuable in later life. The more people he can meet and know, the better off he is.

The Aggie Spirit is something far beyond the realm of my vocabulary. I cannot describe it. The outsider or newcomer, when told about the effects of the Aggie Spirit, tends to think there is nothing to it; but just let him attend a few yell practices and it won't be long 'til he, too, has the Aggie Spirit. You will never find an Aggie who is not more than glad to tell you of his experience with the Spirit. It is something that just gets hold of you and you have cold chills, a cold sweat, a fever, a nervous breakdown, and the biggest thrill of your life all at the same time. Just to hear a corps of 5,500 men yelling as if it were just one huge voice is a thrill beyond description by words. Yell practice is held on the "Y" steps every night after supper during the football season. They have been holding yell practice on this very same spot for over twenty-five years.

Another tradition of all Aggies is to travel by hitch-hiking. It is hard to find an Aggie who hasn't at some time or another gone somewhere on his thumb. The driver of a car need not fear that his car will be swamped if he stops to pick up some boys when there are some forty or fifty boys standing beside the road, because, according to tradition and the Aggie system, the boys in line are numbered and only the number of boys the driver indicates he can carry will go to his car. Hitch-hiking is not only an adventure, but is also educational. One has the opportunity of making some splendid contacts, and of exchanging views with all classes of people. People do not mind helping an Aggie for they know he is clean, courteous, intelligent and grateful for any kindness which might be shown him. This attitude should indicate the power of tradition.

On Thanksgiving Day, the seniors hold a traditional walk down Military Walk. This is to signify the last path of a dying elephant and is therefore named the "Elephant Walk." All of the seniors throw aside their dignity and authority, pull out their shirt-tails, take off their ties, and form what looks like a long snake winding down Military Walk.

Fish Day is the day when the College is more or less put in the hands of the freshman class. They command the companies, send upperclassmen on details, and "rate" over everyone on the campus. This tradition is one of the oldest on the campus.

The social season at A&M is composed of a series of organization dances. Each military organization has a prom sometime between the Christmas holidays and the Final

Review. Some of the organizations have been having these annual balls for some twenty or twenty-five years.

Final Review is always held the day following commencement ceremonies. At the Final Review, the Reserve Officer commissions are presented to the graduating cadets. It is the most colorful tradition and ceremony of the year.

I know that this does not include all of the traditions here at Aggieland, but I have only tried to mention the oldest and most important.

Yours very truly,

Elmer Hook

College Station, Texas

Feb. 13, 1940

Dear Joe:

Do you remember last fall my writing you about "Reveille," our mascot? I did not say very much about her at the time as I was too excited about football and such. The other day while in the administration building I met Mr. H.B. McElroy of the Publicity Department who told me all about her. It is a very interesting story so I will tell you about it.

It seems that several Aggies went to Navasota for reasons unknown back in 1931 in the heyday of Model T. Fords. On the return trip they ran over a small puppy in the middle of the road. After discovering that she was not dead, the boys decided to take her to the College and make a pet of her. She was named "Reveille" the morning when she raised such a howl as the reveille bugle blew. To show that she was a good sport she made formation with the boys and sauntered into the Mess Hall later. After a run-in with the waiters, the boys convinced everyone that it was okay for "Rev" to eat with the fellows.

She seemed to like the band music so she was taken to a football game a few days later. When the famous Aggie Band marched onto the field the spectators were amused to see a small puppy capering in front of the band leaders. From that day on, Texas A&M had a mascot.

It is a tradition now that the head yell leader buys a blanket for her each year. At the end of the year he keeps the blanket which he cherishes very much. She makes most of the close corps trips, riding like a queen in the coaches. On one of these corps trips a conductor made the mistake of trying to throw her off the train because she was occupying an entire seat while some of the passengers were compelled to stand.

He never made that mistake again for immediately a group of Aggies were upon him and nearly tossed him off instead.

Another very interesting thing about "Reveille" is that she has no favorites among the fellows. She has a free range of all buildings and dormitories on the campus and should she decide to sleep in some Aggie's bunk for the night, all she has to do is make herself comfortable and that particular Aggie has to find himself another sleeping place for the night. Woe be unto him if he tries to make her leave his bunk.

Oh, yes! I almost forgot. She still prefers the open Model T. to the Packard. She stands on the back seat with her forefeet on the rear of the front seat and barks louder than the noise of the car as it rambles along.

You should have seen her last fall when Baylor played A&M. She was in her glory then for her favorite playmate, Joe College, the black bear mascot from Baylor was paying her a visit. My M.E. instructor took some movies of them before the game started and between halves when the bands performed.

I thought you would be interested in knowing more about our one and only mascot.

Give my regards to you mother and the rest of the family.

Your friend, Elmer

College Station, Texas

Feb. 20, 1940

Dear Mom:

I was glad to get your letter and to know that you are all getting along fine. And I think you were sweet, Mom, to send me the candy. I passed it around to some of the fellows, and they all wanted a second piece. However, I managed to get away with several pieces, and so I stuffed them down in my pockets Sunday afternoon and went for a long walk. It's nice to have something to nibble on when you're taking a walk with no place in particular to end up.

This walk was rather different than most, though, for my friend and I came upon a rather strange sight. It was a house divided in half with only a small space separating the two parts. We learned that it was the "Believe It or Not" house. You see, a couple by the names of Curtis and Rosetta Cheeks once lived in this small ordinary looking house out beyond College Park Addition. It seems that they "just couldn't agree," as the old husband told us, so they decided to separate. They couldn't even agree on who should have the house, so they just sawed the house in two parts and moved them a little ways apart. Robert L. Ripley gave the

"Divorced House" so much publicity that a Hollywood moving picture company took shots of it for a short "Believe It or Not" feature.

But this is not the only oddity here. Ripley once carried an article in his column about Sbisa Hall being the largest eating establishment in the world. It will seat 2,800 Aggies at one time. The Aggieland Inn was also mentioned in his column as being the only government owned hotel in the world.

Also, A&M was brought to the attention of Ripley by the very unusual incident of a mule giving birth to a colt. One can expect anything here!

Thanks in advance for your next box of candy, Mom.

With love,
Elmer

College Station, Texas

March 2, 1940

Dear Bud:

You know how we Aggies feel about the teasipper from the University of Texas. Well, last year during the Texas A&M basketball game at the Gym, "Tea for Two" was played by the band as the editor and sports editor of the Daily Texan were served tea between halves. The two Texas students were covering the game for the University's paper. The Aggies hated to see them suffer the lack of their customary beverage.

Incidentally, the Longhorns beat the Aggies 41-37 and the last laugh was on the Aggies that time, but we are really waiting for them this year—and I think we'll take them. They are tied with Rice for top place in the Southwest Conference.

We would rather beat those sissies than any other team in the conference, so keep your radio tuned to the game on Saturday night. I don't have any more time just now but I will give you a detailed account of the game later.

Regards to the rest of the family,

Elmer

College Station, Texas

March 5, 1940

Dear Bud:

I told you we would take the teasippers in our basketball games. Well, we took them to the count of two Saturday night. The "Little Army" or the Aggie "Fish" started the ball rolling with a 30-14 trouncing of the Texas Yearlings. Following this, the Aggies played championship ball in defeating the Longhorns by the slim margin of one point and this in closing seconds of the game. The first half was all Army as the Varsity methodically built up a load of 11 points by the end of the half. The teams left the floor with A&M on top to the tune of 33 to 22. During intermission the A&M Tumbling Team entertained the crowd with a very good program of gymnastics. Those boys are real good, I mean. They did some very hard acrobatic stunts that showed many long hours of practice.

Texas came back with a bang after the half way mark and gradually overtook the Aggies within ten minutes. The lead see-sawed during the remainder of the game with the count 51 all only a few minutes before the end of the game. Our hearts sank to a new depth when an Aggie fouled a steer and he made a good free throw to put them ahead 52-51. With only seconds to go, Charlie Stevenson, an Aggie substitute, shot a perfect goal from the center of the floor. The crowd really went wild as the gun went off a few seconds later. We kept Texas from winning and boy, were we glad.

After the game some of us went out to Ed's to celebrate the victory. Some Texas sissies were out there bleeding about the way the game ended, and making their company most unwelcomed. Two of them tried to pick a fight with a football player, who happened to be one of the Southwestern All-Conference players. He made short work of them by bumping their heads together and throwing them out by himself. This seemed to dampen their enthusiasm for we were not bothered with them anymore.

You know it will not be very long until the Spring holidays and I will be glad. I am going to have a date every night while I am home. Shall we double date as we used to do? This all-male Army stuff is okay, but my, how you long to take a girl in your arms and feel the warmth of her personality against your manly chest as you brush her lips with kisses. Pardon my getting mushy but I am merely living in anticipation of things that I hope will come to pass and if they do not, it will not be my fault.

Dreaming again,

Elmer

College Station, Texas

March 7, 1940

Dear Joe:

I remember promising to write you about my first corps dance. Well, spring is here, and boy, how well a guy knows it when these dances start bobbing up every weekend! I suppose there is more than one reason why they give so many dances in the spring of the year—but unless I miss my guess, they didn't overlook the fact that a girl away from home on a balmy night with an Aggie—well, you know the rest of the details. A dark campus bench along with that old spring get-together feeling! Any guy would know that's the best time of the year for social gatherings.

The first of these time honored functions it was my pleasure to attend was the corps dance following the Field Artillery ball. Was it a pip! I was really looking forward to a full evening as I didn't have a date. I had resolved myself to a night of "bird dogging," which, by the way, is a well-apportioned name that denotes a male on the loose, or rather an ambitious stag!

One thing that is sure to happen when there are more males than females—some male is going to get stung!

I used to think some girls were pretty, but since I've been down here, my standards have been revised and they are a good bit more flexible. If I look long enough at any girl now, I can find something that is of human interest. On my arrival at this, my first corps dance, I began applying my new standards—and my eyes! All of a sudden, I saw a girl who gave me a flirtatious wink as she danced by—zoom! Before I scarcely realized it, I followed the old magnetic pull and was tagging in. Gosh, she was a responsive little blond! I didn't find that out until at least five minutes later when she started dancing close. One thing led to another, and you can guess what happened. We both got sorta warm in the dance hall, and through a mutual agreement decided to drift off the floor and out on the campus. I hated to stop dancing with her because she was dancing so close that I could feel everything that makes up the front part of a well developed girl, and she put up a good front!

It was a lovely night and things seemed to be pretty much under control, so together we picked out a secluded bench and talked—and, well, you know how one thing leads to another and she didn't seem to mind, so I kept trying to bring the problem to equilibrium! Well—suppose you know there's an answer to all problems, engineering, or otherwise, so she up and states the solution and back to the dance we started! However, it was a good thing we did, for the last number was just starting.

Well, dogs aren't the most mistreated creatures after all, and I still say some males always get stung!! In Aggie language, maybe he was—

"My Old Lady" did not fare so well as I at the dance. He had a blind date and wow—was she homely! She was the tallest, ill-proportioned, ugliest girl I, or any of the other fellows had seen in the state of Texas, which is noted for its beautiful women. You should have seen them dancing together—he is short and rather thin, and she was just the opposite. You can bet your boots that I didn't spend any time "bird dogging" him.

I wish you could have seen him after intermission. He was a sight! His face was scratched, and he had a large "hickey" above his right eye. His story was a scream. He swears that they walked down to the Administration building during intermission and that she dared him to swing on the flag pole rope, which he did. He says the bruises, etc. were caused when he swung out too far and fell in the hedge surrounding the flag pole. Of course, that's his story and he sticks to it—but we fellows have other ideas. However, he had the consolation of winning the jack-pot for having the ugliest girl. You see, we fellows all chipped in a quarter each before the blind dates arrived. After the dance was over, a meeting was held to vote on the ugliest date. The voting was 100 percent for "My Old Lady" and he is $10 better off, even if he did end up with a knot on his head. After he won it, I didn't feel so bad about having to chip in a quarter when I didn't have a date. I got my quarter back with interest, for he took me out for a feed on part of the winnings.

Guess I'd better get to studying.

Your friend,
Elmer

College Station, Texas

March 11, 1940

Dear Mom,

Guess what! I have made the "Singing Cadets," the A&M Glee Club. It is a very distinguished organization composed of the outstanding singers on the campus, and I consider myself lucky to be a member. We are planning several trips to Houston, Waco, Dallas and other surrounding cities, where we will appear at various civic clubs, high schools and A&M Mothers' Clubs. We sing religious songs, popular songs, and of course "The Aggie War Hymn" and "The Spirit of Aggieland."

Mom, if you have a chance to read "The American Legion Magazine," read Bill Cunningham's story about A&M "And What A College." I think you will be very much impressed with his article as all of us were. He told about the achievements of the college, its outstanding graduates, our championship football team, the "Twelfth Man" and numerous other things I don't have time to mention. In closing he wrote, *"Its football team indeed was great, but it is really only catching up with the rich service in peace, the gallant record in war, and the potential bulwark if our national honor or safety is definitely challenged in the future that makes this one of the distinctive institutions of the entire United States. Yeah, Aggies!"* Was that not a noble challenge to us Aggies? We are trying to live up to the heritage which is ours.

I suppose you read in the paper the article written by Dale Carnegie concerning the Project Houses here at A&M. Just in case you failed to see it, I will outline briefly the co-operative House plan established here by Dr. Daniel Russell, Professor of Rural Sociology. Several years ago, Dr. Russell and twelve students found a deserted haunted house, a large two story building near the College's experiment farm. This house was furnished with articles from the boys' own homes. The boys did most of the work, cleaned their own rooms, set tables, washed dishes, cutting expense to a minimum. From this start has grown the student cooperative housing project, the largest organization of its kind in the United States. There are now 1,000 boys attending A&M on approximately $17.00 per month who stay in the Project Houses. The $23,000 American Legion Hall that houses eighty-four boys is included in this plan.

I mentioned these things as I know you are always interested in the unique things about Aggieland.

Your son, Elmer

College Station, Texas

March 15, 1940

Dear Tom:

I have my work up to date and have decided to come home next weekend. If I get there in time, we ought to double date Saturday night and go dancing. Don't expect me too early, though, as I might get caught on the road and be too late to go. Of course, I should be able to get there by six o'clock, but you never can tell. I think I told you before that hitch-hiking is the major mode of transportation for the Aggies. I've gone quite a few places that way this year, and it's been a lot of fun.

Sometimes it is pretty hard to get a ride, I think the easiest time of it for me was when I started to New Orleans for the Sugar Bowl game. That was just a breeze! About the worst trip I've had was to Fort Worth one weekend. I left here at two o'clock and didn't get to Cow Town until five the next morning. It was cold and rainy all the way, and there were quite a few of the fellows going up. We had to build fires on the side of the road several places to try to keep warm.

It takes longer to catch a ride when there are a number of Aggies ahead of you. Whenever there is more than one person, each Aggie numbers off. Then all but the first fellow stands off, and he tries to catch a ride. If a car comes by destined for some place which would be out of the way for the first fellow, then the next down the line can take the ride if he likes.

You see, we have specific rules governing the "open road." It's against the rules to "upstream" boys trying to catch a ride. Of course, "downstream" is ok for then the crowd gets first chance at a ride.

It's also in the rules that we should try to be company to anyone who may ask us to ride. By that I mean that the Aggies are instructed to always try to carry on a good conversation, for a lot of men, like salesmen, etc., pick up boys just to have someone to keep them company. I think it can be said of most of the fellows that they try to be courteous and friendly to any person who might give them a lift. Sometimes the person who picks you up will ask you to drive for him, and certainly no Aggie who can drive would think of refusing.

I supposed you are wondering how these rules of the road can be enforced. They may not always be kept strictly, but when an Aggie gets caught disobeying them, it's just too bad. A sophomore caught a "Fish" "up streaming" in Dallas about two weeks ago, and for a week after that the "Fish" had difficulty in sitting down comfortably.

One of the boys here won quite a bit of publicity by his hitch-hiking feat. I guess that you read about the jaunt Keyes Carson took from coast to coast last summer.

Well, Tom, I guess I'd better stop this letter right here and get some studying done for classes tomorrow. I'll try to see you late Saturday afternoon.

Your friend,

Elmer

College Station, Texas

March 18, 1940

Dear Mom:

I promised to write and tell you all about the dance last weekend. Well, the time we had all looked forward to had finally come—the day of the Engineer's Ball. I never saw a happier bunch of boys in my life, except those who didn't have dates. Everyone was packing his things, getting ready to move out of the dorm. I think I told you how arrangements were made for the girls. The boys sign up for rooms for their girls in the Commandant's office, and have everything fixed up and ready for the girls to move in. The boys who vacate their rooms have to stay anywhere they can, and that means mostly everywhere. Besides, we hardly went to bed anyway that weekend, so it doesn't make much difference.

The girls began arriving a little before noon. There were a few who came in that morning, but most of them got here on the noon bus. About 4 o'clock the campus was swarming with cute girls. We always have had the reputation of having the prettiest girls down, and I think we held it up 100 percent this year.

Some of the companies had banquets that night before the Ball. We had ours in the banquet room of the mess hall. Besides good food, the banquets serve as a sort of ice-breaker. The banquet was over about 8:30 and the dance started at 9 o'clock. We had George Hamilton and his orchestra down to play for us, and he was great! His orchestra is tops in rhumbas and tangos. The dance was over at one o'clock, and everyone was pretty tired out. However, the girls didn't have to be in until three, so couples scattered over the campus. No one would think of taking a girl in before the time limit is up— unless she has been a wallflower all evening!

Saturday morning we all had a pretty hard time waking up, but when we finally got up, it didn't take us long to dress and go get the girls. Saturday was spent loafing. Some had picnics, some went to the Bryan Country Club and danced, and some just sat around. It was a warm spring day and perfect for loafing. Most everyone went to the corps dance Saturday night and had a swell time.

Finally, Sunday came— the day for the girls to leave. You could tell it for everywhere you looked you could see boys with faces a mile long. Sunday night seemed dead and lonesome, like the calm after the storm, but we all went to sleep with memories of a happy and wonderful weekend.

Well, Mom, I guess Sue will come by and tell you all about it anyway. I sure was glad I asked her down for the weekend because we had a swell time together.

With love,

Elmer

College Station, Texas

March 28, 1940

Dear Mom and Dad:

Did you read about the storm we had here at school the other day? It came up so suddenly, we were all caught with our pants down. The sky was slightly overcast at noon but everyone went to the post office as usual. On the way back to my "hole" I noticed it was getting darker so I ran to the dorm to get my math book and close my windows. Then I had to hurry back to the Academic building to meet class. Well sir, a little after one o'clock, the wind really hit the building with a bang. We were working problems at the board when the lights went out. They came on, flickered a while, and then went off again. The teacher allowed us to go to the window to watch the storm, and while he wasn't looking, someone snapped the light switch so that the lights would not turn on again when the power came on. It was about fifteen minutes later before the instructor noticed that the rest of the building was lighted.

During this time the wind continued to get stronger, bending the trees to the ground. I happened to think of one of my friends — George, about whom I have written you. He is taking a course in aviation and was scheduled to fly that particular afternoon. As we were watching the wind get stronger, we suddenly heard a racing motor and saw a plane dart over at a terrific speed. I was really scared then, and I could hardly wait until class was over to see if my friend had been in the air during the storm.

Of course I was anxious to know what had happened so I rushed outside to find that the news of the planes was already out. Everyone was talking of how George and another Aggie were up flying when the storm started. The instructor was unable to give them the proper signals from the ground, so he decided to go up in another plane and show them how to land. Just as he took off, George and the other student flying managed to land safely. The instructor tried to land also, but by this time the storm really hit and the force of the wind prevented his landing. He finally had to turn the plane which we had seen from the window. He finally managed to land in a field about five miles from the college. A farmer saw him and thinking there had been a wreck, he telephoned Bryan and had the ambulance sent out. You know how suddenly a storm can be over. Well, as neither the instructor nor the plane was hurt in any way, he was able to take off about thirty minutes later and flew back to the airport, and the ambulance rushed out to the farm to find that he had already gone. Of course, it was funny to everyone but the ambulance driver. We were all pretty scared for a while.

Say, Dad, I wonder if you could let me have a little money now before the end of the month? I really need it badly.

Love,

Elmer

College Station, Texas

April 5, 1940

Dear Joe:

Postmaster General James A. Farley was on the campus yesterday — and did we greet him royally.

We met him with a Cavalry Escort at the Main Entrance to the campus, gave him a nineteen gun salute, presented a formal review of the entire cadet corps and feted him to the largest banquet ever held in Sbisa Hall.

The high spot of the mounted full-dress review was the introduction of all the seniors to General Farley. At the banquet, which incidentally was attended by some 1,000 odd students, faculty members and distinguished visitors, "Jo-Jo" White, senior letterman of the famous Aggie football team presented Mr. Farley with a white football autographed with the signatures of the entire football squad of 1939-40. General Farley seemed to be very much pleased with the gift. He said he had listened to the entire Sugar Bowl classic when the Aggies defeated Tulane for the national championship. By the way, he gave a very interesting address on politics and such.

Well, April Fool's Day slipped by without any pranks being pulled on the Profs. The Aggies used to tear everything loose on that day. Some sort of agreement was made about holidays or something; anyway we missed a lot of fun, or grief, or both as they seem to go hand in hand.

In the past, the fellows have really taken things over. They would carry alarm clocks to classes and have them set to go off at different times. Some of their parades were coworkers I am told.

Your friend,

Elmer

College Station, Texas

April 10, 1940

Dear Bill:

You should have been out on Kyle Field last Saturday
to witness A&M's first Minor Sports Festival. One of the
highlights of the day was the match between the Texas State
College for Women Rifle Team and the A&M Rifle Team, 1940
winners of the Hearst Trophy in the 8th Corps Area. The first
match was won by the Aggies by a score of 784 to 725. The
boys then gave the girls from Denton a 40-point handicap and
a second match was fired which the girls won by the score of
514 to 487.

The news services carried accounts of the matches on
their broadcasts Saturday night. Ann Sheridan, Hollywood's
"Oomph Girl," who was listening in, immediately wired her
congratulations in such a nice way that I am enclosing her
message.

Telegram

"I rejoice that the spirit of gallantry still lives in Texas.

"It was wonderful for A&M Rifle Team to shoulder an undue handicap in order that their fair visitors would outshoot them.

"To the Rifle Team of A&M and to the cadet corps of 6,000 gentlemen I send affectionate congratulations and regards.

"Look for me in your yelling section when A&M plays UCLA in October."

Cordially yours,
Ann Sheridan

As you know, Miss Sheridan is a native of Texas. Her telegraphed congratulations started a beautiful friendship with the boys at Texas A&M. Perhaps you noticed in the papers several weeks ago the article written by the Harvard Lampoon Movie Critic in which he chose likely to succeed. The editor of the Yale Recorder to up the defense of the "Oomph Girl" from Denton, Texas. He challenged the editor of the Harvard Lampoon to a duel "European Code." The Harvard editor replied that if he had to fight a duel, his choice of weapons would be the telegraph — at 155 miles. We Aggies, being more gallant, too up the defense of this truly capable Texas girl in the traditional Army fashion. Our challenges do not include such panty-waist weapons as the telegraph. Our National Championship Football Team will carry the challenge to the gridiron — our Intercollegiate Champion Pistol-Team will take pistols at fifty paces — our 8th Corps Area Champion Rifle Team will even allow a handicap to anyone at 100 yards — while the remainder of us 6,000 Aggies will revert to our old fists at any old tie in the defense of "the bell who HAS succeeded in the hearts of Aggies everywhere." Such is the sentiment of the Army, so aptly expressed by the pens of Backwash columnist, George Fuermann, and the editor of **The Battalion**, Bill Murray.

Watch the papers for further developments.

Sincerely your friend,

Elmer

College Station, Texas

April 18, 1940

Dear Joe:

I suppose you have the impression that A&M is a hell-raising school after reading all of the letters I wrote last semester.

I tried to tell you about a few of the traditions that have made A&M the school it is today. Being a green "Fish' I was naturally very much impressed by the various activities we had to perform our first semester on the campus.

Now that the second semester is under way we have settled down to do some real studying. I have been planning to tell you something about the School of Engineering. We are fortunate in having a former State Highway Engineer, Mr. Gibb Gilchrist, as our Dean. Speaking of the Dean, several of the boys in our Battery make the Dean's team last semester. I was very fortunate in making good grades so I was not called down to his office. However, I understand there is one consolation in visiting his office. He has a beautiful brunette for his stenographer. She surely is a peach!

Did you know we have the second largest Engineering School in the United States? You can pursue almost any kind of engineering you desire. The following curricula are offered in the School of Engineering: Four-year courses of study in Architectural Engineering, Chemical Engineering, Civil Engineering, Electrical Engineering, Engineering Administration, Industrial Education, Industrial Engineering, Mechanical Engineering, Petroleum Engineering, and Aeronautical Engineering; five-year courses of study in Architecture, Petroleum Engineering, Mechanical and Petroleum Engineering.

Our Mechanical Engineering Department is tops. We have some professors who are outstanding in the field of engineering. The Head of the Department, Professor C.W. Crawford, is very prominent in engineering circles. He wrote the "Introductory Problems in Engineering" which we use as a text our year. This book is the foundation upon which all of our future work in engineering is built. We have an excellent opportunity to study heating, ventilating and air-conditioning and the school is very fortunate having Dr. F. E. Giesecke, President of the American Society of Heating and Ventilating Engineers as Professor Emeritus in this department. Two other men in this department, Professors V.M. Faires and A.V. Brewer, have written several texts and problem books on Applied Thermodynamics which are used in thirty or forty different engineering schools. Professor Faires has written other books which are widely used, especially his books on "Machine Design." He is also very active in the Student Branch of the American Society of Mechanical Engineers.

Dr. Frank C. Bolton, Vice President and Dean of the College and Professor of Electrical Engineering, is an officer in the American Institute of Electrical Engineers and a well-known authority on electrical engineering subjects.

If you will take a glance at the nationally known engineering graduates of Texas A&M, you will see why we are so enthusiastic over our school.

If you are interested in enrolling in the School of Engineering, I would suggest your writing for one of the college catalogs which will explain in detail the courses of study available.

My address is the same so write me when you have time.

Elmer

P.S. Tuesday noon, an announcement was made over the amplifying systems of the dining halls to the effect that an Aggie was critically ill and in very urgent need of a blood transfusion. The announcers asked that all Aggies who were willing to give their blood to their fellow Aggie to report to the hospital immediately. Within fifteen minutes, 250 of us boys had reported to the hospital to offer our blood. Before the afternoon had passed more than 400 had volunteered. The Aggie's brother was the first to actually give blood as his count was nearest his brother's. Several others were placed on the list in case other transfusions were needed. Where else in the United States or any place as far as that goes will you find such esprit de corps?

E.H.

College Station, Texas
April 19, 1940

Dear John:

I've just come back from the observance of the most beautiful and impressive of all the Aggie customs and traditions — "Silver Taps."

This custom of having a group of trumpeters play taps in harmony from the top of the Academic Building at eleven o'clock at night while the whole corps stands at attention, is usually observed when an Aggie dies or is killed. It is the Aggies' way of paying final tribute to a buddy — it's the Aggies' last goodbye to a friend.

But this is not the only time that the custom is observed. The night before leave for the Christmas Holidays is given, "Silver Taps" and **Home Sweet Home** are played. The notes seem to have a more cheerful ring then as they float out over the campus for everyone is happy and filled with thoughts of Christmas and home.

Tonight the trumpets blended their beautiful harmony for James W…of X Coast Artillery, who died yesterday from injuries received in an auto wreck last weekend. Believe me, John it's a real thrill to see that huge mass of Aggies, nearly

6,000 in all, standing at attention there in the moonlight —
Aggies dress only in pajamas and bathrobes, some fully
dressed and some clad in house slippers and underwear. The
biggest thrill of all comes, though, as the actual "Silver Taps"
come drifting over the stillness, seemingly from nowhere. The
night is warm, but you kinda feel cold along your spine and
you can't help but repeat the words to yourself as you listen —

"Day is done, Gone the sun

From the hill, form the lake, from the sky.

All is well, safely rest,

God is nigh."

You really do have a feeling that "God is nigh" as you
hear that music. Aw, maybe I'm just a sentimentalist!
Anyway, John, I thought you'd be interested in hearing about
this — the most beautiful of all Aggie customs — "Silver Taps."

Yours truly,

Elmer

College Station, Texas

April 29, 1940

Dear Joe:

Well, I imagine that you have heard about our new stay-at-home program. In other words, we can't go to shows in Bryan; in fact, we can't even go to Bryan unless we get a pass signed by a senior and you really have to have a good reason before you can get the pass. Everyday a number of seniors are in Bryan to see that this is complied with.

Last Saturday night, I had a date with a girl who lived in Bryan. I had made the date before this business came up, and since I dislike to break a date, I decided to go on and keep it.

When you have a date in Bryan and don't have a car, there is only one thing to do and that is to go to the show. That gave me two big problems; namely, how to get into Bryan unseen and above all, how to get into the show. I had to wear my uniform too, because it is a very serious offense to be caught non-reg in Bryan, and a time like this makes uniforms stand out like sore thumbs.

Luckily for me, my date lived near the railroad tracks, which ran directly behind the show. I just happened to recall that there was a gap between the theater and the building next door. All the fire exits opened into this gap, which is about four feet wide and runs the length of the building. I had the capital idea of arranging to have tickets mailed to me with permission to come in through one of the fire exits. So the only problem left was a means of getting into Bryan, and I finally decided that the only thing to do was to catch the 7:30 freight, which goes through here and also passes through Bryan.

Everything worked out just as I had planned except for one thing. My date and I walked down the tracks until we were behind the show and were admitted as per arrangement.

I happened to glance toward the back of the show and there stood a senior. Boy, was I scared! I just melted into my seat. I don't suppose he saw me, as nothing was said about it; however, that was the longest show I have ever seen, or at least it seemed so. That was one Saturday night I was really glad to get back to my little room. It was really an adventure, but I don't believe I'll ever try anything like that again. I was too lucky! From now on, I'm a law abiding citizen—can you believe it?

But I did think it was pretty smart of the old bean to devise such a sly method of putting one over on the rulers of this land. However, I can't hold a candle to the ingenuity of some of these Aggies. Some of the stunts that are pulled in this place are corkers! Of course, a bull session is the place to tell you about some of the pranks, but "My Old Lady" wrote a theme in English 103 the other day on the subject of various pranks played by the fellows and he has given me leave to send it along with this letter. I told him you'd get a big kick out of reading it.

Write me soon.

Your friend,

Elmer

P.S. Speaking of different ways of courting; one of the juniors in "B" Company Signal Corps, Jack Hines, has been broadcasting and receiving messages over his short-wave radio set from our sister school, TSCW. Travis Little, a co-ed from the Denton school, operating on the call number of W5AAN, is Dan Cupid's first hand assistant at that Institute of Beautiful Women. They have received nationwide publicity as a result of their numerous messages over the air waves. I understand they send about fifty messages per week.

E.H.

Theme Pranks

During a school year here at A&M, there are things which happen by chance, or by well-laid plans, that demand a sense of humor for the proper appreciation. In fact, there are some of the fellows, especially "Fish," who spend quite a bit of time and thought on the feat of making another fellow both ridiculous and uncomfortable. Of course, it is all in the spirit of good fun and I guess I'd begin to feel left out if someone did not remember to drown me out once in a while gross indignities, such as holding up the wall and duck-walking around the room, tend to inspire pranks on the upperclassmen. The "Fish" have to be subtle and under-cover with any sort of revenge. My first prank was what I title "the syrup episode." On one of my hitch-hiking trips, a fellow who picked me up gave me a can of his special carrot juice syrup, which, he said, was a special invention of his. Later, I was glad I accepted the can of syrup for my inventive mind found a swell use for it. I took my can of syrup and slipped into the gun room. With all seriousness and deliberation, I poured some of the splendid carrot juice syrup down the barrel of my favorite sophomore's gun. I flipped the bolt a couple of times, just to ensure a good job, and then slipped out of the gun room unseen and very proud of my idea. It was sweet revenge several days later when the sophomore had to walk the bull ring for two sessions because rifle inspection disclosed the because rifle inspection disclosed the presence of the ill-smelling syrup! When my conscience hurts me, I comfort myself with the thought that I might have put the stuff in his bed instead of his gun, and that would have been more uncomfortable.

One night just before Christmas when fireworks were going off all over the campus, I slipped into the room of a D Battery "Fish" and tied a string to the screen. Then the string was run to a point about a hundred feet away from the building and with the use of an eye hook, a skyrocket was attached to the string. When the D Battery "Fish" got to his room that night and went to bed, my pal and I set the skyrocket off and watched for the fun. It went up the string faster and faster, until by the time it had reached the screen, it was traveling with a tremendous velocity. Boy, it didn't stop at the screen — it went right into the room, landed on the top bunk and exploded there, throwing a shower of multicolored sparks all over the room. The victim yelled bloody murder, and he was weak for several days from the fright we gave him!

The old custom of "drowning out" is practiced a great deal at A&M, but three other "Fish" and myself got together one day to devise a plan to take care of a particularly superior senior. We sneaked into his room and removed all light globes and inside door knobs, leaving the senior without lights or any means of escape when the door was closed. We had to work quietly so as not to wake him, but we had everything planned to the minute so it worked swell. All four of us had large buckets of water which we dumped onto the bed in unison. As we ran out, we slammed the door behind us. The senior set up a howl, but we didn't get caught. We ducked into our rooms, and to bed to discuss the very pleasant subject of how the proud senior was left in his room for the rest of the night without lights or a means of escape, and with only a hard chair, the floor or a soaked mattress to sleep on.

Some pranks are played without previous plans. Sometimes the impromptu type are the best. For instance, soon after school started this year, a certain Coast Artillery captain was suffering from a slight cold. Just before retiring, he sent to his first sergeant for some cold pills. Instead of cold pills, the top kick sent him some sort of pills that caused him to urinate green. The next morning when the captain discovered what had happened to him, he got his board and promptly paid the first sergeant a visit.

Over in C Battery one day a "Fish" captured an alley cat and fed it a box of Ex-Lax. He then proceeded to put the cat on the bed in another "Fish's" room and locked the door. When the unsuspecting "Fish" returned he found the sleeping Tabby and a sight which would be a convincing recommendation of the regularity and effectiveness of Ex-Lax.

There is also the story about the purebred goat that was given to A&M for experimental purposes by one of the more prominent figures in the State. Following the delivery of the goat, it is said that officials of the College received a letter which said in part: "I am sending my children to the University of Texas and in order that A&M will not feel slighted, I am sending Billy, my purebred goat, to A&M." It seems that some of the students misinterpreted the donor's intentions, and what happened to Billy is a sad, sad story, at least to Billy. Under cover of night, a group of unidentified but prankful "Vet" students went to work on Billy and robbed him of his glorious heritage, thereby making him a sort of wallflower among the goat herd. Of course the goat recovered from the unauthorized operation, but I guess his face gets pretty long when he thinks of what might have been a very eventful future. Billy is still a fine purebred goat, but considering the turn of events and his social decline, he may not think a college education pays.

Last year there was a popular song "I Must See Annie Tonight," which was the source of a lot of worry to the telephone operator. The song was played in every night spot around here, and as the Aggies get around a lot, they naturally heard the part about "hello, central, give me a line, I'm calling Bryan (t) 709." The "t" wasn't very clear, so most fellows thought the line giving the trouble was Bryan 709. Well, by the time all the Aggies had called Bryan 709 it ceased to be funny to the person who always answered the phone. After receiving hundreds of calls, the office boy yelled over the wire in desperation: "Hell no, Annie doesn't live here and never has — this is the City Warehouse and Shop!" There were so many calls the telephone company changed the number.

College Station, Texas

May 4, 1940

Dear Bill:

Well, here it is near the end of school and I have practically completed my "Fish" year at Texas A&M.

We had our "Fish Day" a few days age, so I really am not considered a "Fish" anymore. It is a tradition that the "Fish" of each organization run things for the entire day. The upperclassmen clean up the "Fish's" rooms in the morning, wait on the "Fish" at meals, run details throughout the day, etc. In fact, the "Fish" take over. A party usually closes the day. I'll tell you more in detail when I see you.

I have a little time so I will finish telling you about the Ann Sheridan episode I started to relate several weeks ago. A special committee composed of Coach Homer Norton, All-American John Kimbrough, Waleman"Cotton" Price, Ernie Pannell, and columnist George Fuermann went to Dallas to present an autographed football to Miss Sheridan. It so happened that Texas Ann was in bed with the flu so the football was presented to American Airline hostess Norman Fredrickson, who in turn presented it to Miss Sheridan upon her arrival in **Los Angeles**. The football carried the autographs of the entire national championship squad and an inscription inviting Miss Sheridan to be the official hostess and sponsor on their trip to the West Coast next fall when they play UCLA. At this writing, nothing definite has been heard from Miss Sheridan, but we feel sure that she will accept the invitation.

Speaking of the UCLA game next October, we are going to make the trip. Boy, I bet you wish you could toot a horn and that you were an A&M student. We are already planning the show we will put on. My, my! Will we have a time! To top everything else, we are going to have dates with Warner Bros.' attractive extras who are going to form an all-female yelling section giving our famous Aggies yells. It just sounds too good to be true, but it's the truth. Warner Brother's publicity agents, Bill Lewis and Henry Krumm, instigated the plan which gained rapid favor with the corps. Our yell leaders, Buster Keeton and "Foots" Bland and George Fuermann, Backwash columnist of **The Battalion**, are now making final plans with Warner Brothers.

Say, I almost forgot; you may see a full-length movie based on Texas A&M if our luck holds out. We are planning to sign a petition asking Warner Brothers to make a movie about A&M starring Ann Sheridan. I don't know whether a petition of 6,000 Aggies and probably an equal number of alumni will have any weight with Warner Brothers. However, it is a happy thought, and you can't keep us from dreaming even it if is day-dreaming. Miss Sheridan should be able to portray the role of the Aggie sweetheart to perfection. Only time will tell.

The rest of the school year will find me very busy so don't expect too many letters from me between now and June.

Your friend,

Elmer

College Station, Texas

May 10, 1940

Dear Joe:

I must tell you of a very funny incident that happened to a group of us last night. I was invited to a picnic at one of the roadside parks on the other side of Bryan. A group of girls in our gang decided that it was their turn to throw the feed, so they cooked the whole affair up. It was really a swell party. We cooked hot dogs, ate sandwiches, cakes, ice cream and everything imaginable. After we had eaten as much as we could hold we played games, including "Three Deep" which proved rather bad for one of the fellows as he broke his glasses in a head-on collision with another "Fish." Someone suggested we dance, so we carried the portable Victrola which someone so thoughtfully had brought along, to the edge of the highway. You know how smooth and wide the concrete of Texas Highway 6 is! We had lots of fun dancing on the road except we were kept busy hollering, "Car coming from Hearne." This grew tiresome after an hour or more, so we went back to the fire and ate everything that was left after our first go-round. Then we formed a ring around the campfire and sang songs—old, new, school songs, yells, anything some member could think of. The party finally broke up and we headed for Bryan. I was driving a car we had borrowed for the occasion, but one of the "bird dogs" in the crowd was making so much time with my date that I decided to let him drive. So we made the change, but I took the middle of the front seat.

We were just getting underway good when we spied a 'possum running across the road. I yelled for the driver to stop so we could catch the 'possum. In my excitement I opened the door and shoved my date out on the edge of the highway where she landed on some cactus or something equally effective. I caught the 'possum by the tail and threw him back on the highway. I turned around just to see the car nose-dive into an immense ditch bordering the highway. The driver had also decided to take up the chase, so he jumped out, forgetting to leave the car in gear or to apply the brakes. Luckily the bank was soft so the car was not hurt. However, the couple in the rear seat were really surprised to look up just as the car headed for the ditch. The boy made a noble attempt to crawl over the front seat and stop the car, but he was too late. Yes, we captured the 'possum. We tried to back out, only to bury the wheels to the hub in the soft shoulders of the ditch. One of the other cars returned to help us in attempting to rescue the stranded car. This car then went into Bryan and borrowed a chain from the Police and towed us out. But in doing this the clutch of the other car became stuck — or something — and we then had to push the other car into Bryan. My, what a night! No serious damage was done to either car, so we came out okay. We lost the 'possum a few days later when someone turned over the barrel in which we had lodged him.

What we Aggies won't do isn't worth doing.

Your friend,

Elmer

College Station, Texas

May 16, 1940

Dear Mom:

I am sorry you could not stay over to see the Annual Corps Area Commander's Inspection of A&M's **Reserve Officers Training Corps**. The corps had really been preparing for this important event for weeks. We had to undergo inspection in the classrooms as well as on the drill field. Being in the Band, I had an opportunity to watch all of the various units as they paraded before the reviewing stands. We were really good.

Mom, I was so glad to have you visit here during the Engineering Show and Mothers' Day program. It gave you a chance to see the type of school we have here. Were you not impressed with the equipment we have in the laboratories of the Mechanical, Electrical and Petroleum Departments? So you can see why we Aggies are so enthusiastic about the training we receive here. And the Mess Hall, you really enjoyed your meals there, did you not? You made a big hit with the boys too. Thanks a lot for inviting "My Old Lady" out home this summer.

Will write more later,

Love, Elmer

College Station, Texas

May 24, 1940

Dear Joe:

Howdy, Joe. Well, I wanted to tell you how sorry I am that you had to leave while I was engaged with that bull ring. It's a darn nuisance! The bull ring meets every Saturday and Sunday at 2 o'clock and lasts for two hours. We have to march around and around and around, down by the Cavalry stables.

The way to get on the bull ring is to be what is called "Pee-Fish." Of course any upperclassman can get on the bull ring, but it is comprised mostly of erring "Fish" who have received demerits from upperclassmen. The juniors can be rammed only by the seniors, and sophomores only by juniors and seniors, while we "Fish" catch it from the whole lot of them. So you can see why it is that freshmen are so constantly in the limelight. Some of the rams are for really doing things we shouldn't, but most of them are just for the hell of it.

In our dorm, the upperclassmen seem to get a lot of kick out of seeing a "Fish" leave for the bull ring. When a freshman gets over twenty rams, he has to start walking and walks them off four rams an hour until he gets back down to

Twenty rams. Sophomores have to keep theirs at sixteen, juniors at twelve and seniors at eight. The upperclassmen only walk off two rams an hour, but you see, they don't get nearly as many as freshmen do.

The bull ring walkers are supervised by a regular Army Officer and those marching have to wear the Number One uniform. To march at attention for two hours every Saturday and Sunday gets pretty monotonous. I have been on the bull rings for twelve out of the last thirteen weeks. That's really going some! No one can say I don't get my daily dozen and then some.

Write me soon, Elmer

College Station, Texas
June 3, 1940

Dear Mom:

This past week has been a very busy one for us band boys. We gave the Final Concert Thursday afternoon at 4:30. Mom, you should have been down. We really strutted at this concert. We have received so many nice comments that we are almost convinced we are good.

Friday was a very busy day too. We played for the Baccalaureate services in the morning and Commencement exercises in the evening. These two services were very impressive. I wish you could have seen those 690-odd graduates dress in their Number One uniforms as they were presented their diplomas by Mr. F. M. Law, President of the Board of Directors.

The Final Review held today was the most touching scene I have ever witnessed. I can understand now the feeling that was aroused when it was announced that the date was changed to a week earlier. It means so much to everyone, especially the graduating seniors. The day started at 8:30 this morning with the formal presentation of reserve commissions by Brigadier-General W.B. Pyron, Texas National Guard,

Houston. Following that we had the Final Review proper. The entire corps passed in review twice before the reviewing stand. There was such a crowd of people lining the drill field that you would think a big football game was being held. The mothers and friends of the graduating seniors were on hand to congratulate them and to tell them goodbye in a lot of cases. After the parade was over the crowd lingered on—reluctant to leave. We were all very sad and happy at the same time. We realized that we would not see some of the fellows again, especially the graduating members of our organizations. The Captain of our outfit tried to make a farewell speech to us and tears rolled down his cheeks. In fact, all of us had moist eyes as we gripped his hand in farewell. Yes, Final Review is an old, old tradition that stands out above all traditions at Texas A&M.

I must do some studying for I have some final exams to take. I was exempt in three of my classes so I am fairly well prepared on my other subjects.

I'll be seeing you soon.

Love,

Elmer

TEXAS A. & M. COLLEGE, COLLEGE STATION, TEXAS

Watch these boys again next fall when all but 7 return to carry on with that Old Spirit of Aggieland. Traced by All-American "Jarrin John" Kimbrough, the 1940 Aggies will be hard to stop.

June 7, 1940

Dear Mom,
    I have completed my Fish year at Texas A. & M. I am leaving for home within a very few minutes via hitch-hiking. This is the card I was telling you about. Turn it over for a good look at the 1939 National Champs. I'll see you soon, Elmer.

Mrs. John F. Hook

Pilot Point

Texas

About the Author

It was on a crowded subway in New York City when John Pasco decided to apply for an assistantship to the Agricultural and Mechanical College of Texas. A group of Hardin-Simmons College co-eds dressed in the traditional western fashion convinced him that Texas was the only state in the union. The next day, he mailed his application and a few weeks later, he was heading west to start work on his Master's Degree.

A graduate of the University of Kentucky with a Bachelor of Science degree in Mechanical Engineering, he has had experience as an assistant fuel research engineer for the Chesapeake and Oho Railway Company, as a lieutenant in the Civilian Conservation Corps, as engineer and subsequently manager of the stoker department of a company in Richmond, Virginia before going to New York City in the summer of 1939 to handle a stoker exhibit at the New York World's Fair.

He conceived the idea of compiling a series of letters written by a freshman at Texas A&M to his friend back home. "Fish Sergeant" is the result. Some of the letters are purely fictional but the majority have been based on actual experiences as reported by various students at A&M. The

"Fish" who does the honors for this grand old school of the southwest is one Elmer Hook, who began his life as a freshman in that school under the handicap of having been elected to the exalted position of "Fish Sergeant" of his Battery. These letters take "Fish" Hook through his "Fish" year, from his first impressions of the College until he heads home for the summer holidays nine months later. He writes of his experiences of "Fish Sergeant," his reduction to the ranks again after a fight with an officer, his account of the Corps Trip to Fort Worth, a weekend at Texas State College for Women at Denton, Texas, the Band Trip to Arkansas, the Armistice Day Celebration and the SMU football game, his helping to build the bonfire before the University of Texas game, the Christmas party, his trip to New Orleans and the Sugar Bowl Classic in which the Texas Aggies won the national championship over Tulane University, the various organizational dances he attended, Final Review, and numerous other incidents stressing the oldest traditions and customs to which the corps adhere so strictly.

Fish Sergeant

Made in the USA
Columbia, SC
15 January 2018